WAR AND PEACE
BOOK FOUR : 1806

By Leo Tolstoy

War and Peace Book 4
by Leo Tolstoy

Copyright © 2025

All Rights reserved.
No part of this publication may be reproduced, stored in a retrieval system, or transmitted in any form or by any means, electronic, mechanical, photocopying or Otherwise, without the written permission of the publisher.

The author/editor asserts the moral right to be identified as the author/editor of this work.

ISBN: 978-93-94973-49-7

Published by
DOUBLE 9 BOOKS
2/13-B, Ansari Road
Daryaganj, New Delhi - 110002
info@double9books.com
www.double9books.com
Tel. 011-40042856

This book is under public domain

Printed in India.

About the Author

Leo Tolstoy was a Russian creator known for his books War and Peace which is viewed as the best book of pragmatist fiction. Tolstoy is additionally viewed as world's best author by quite a few people. Additionally an ethical scholar and a social reformer, Tolstoy had extreme moralistic points of view. In later life, he turned into an intense Christian rebel and anarcho-conservative.

Leo Tolstoy Born in Yasnaya Polyana on September 9, 1828, He had a place with a notable honorable Russian family. He was the fourth among five offspring of Count Nikolai Ilyich Tolstoy and Countess Mariya Tolstaya, both of whom kicked the bucket passing on their youngsters to be raised by family members.

In 1844, Tolstoy was acknowledged into Kazan University. Incapable to graduate past the subsequent year, Tolstoy got back to Yasnava Polyana and afterward invested energy going among Moscow and St. Petersburg. With some functioning information on a few dialects, he turned into a multilingual. Yet again the recently observed youth pulled in Tolstoy towards drinking, visiting massage parlors and most betting which left him in weighty obligation and anguish however Tolstoy before long acknowledged he was carrying on with a brutish life and endeavored college tests with the expectation that he would acquire a situation with the public authority, yet finished yet up in Caucuses serving in the military continuing in the strides of his senior sibling.

In Year 1862, Leo Tolstoy wedded Sophia Andreevna Behrs, generally called Sonya, who was 16 years more youthful than him. The couple had thirteen youngsters, of which, five passed on at an early age. Sonya went about as Tolstoy's secretary, editor and monetary chief while he made two out of his most prominent works. Their initial wedded life was loaded up with happiness.

He started composing his show-stopper, War and Peace in 1862. The six volumes of the work were distributed somewhere in the range of 1863 and 1869. With 580 characters got from history and others made by Tolstoy, this extraordinary novel takes on investigating the hypothesis of history and the irrelevance of noted figures like Alexander and Napoleon. Anna Karenina, Tolstoy's next epic was begun in 1873 and distributed totally in 1878.

Contents

BOOK FOUR : 1806

CHAPTER I	9
CHAPTER II	17
CHAPTER III	23
CHAPTER IV	28
CHAPTER V	33
CHAPTER VI	36
CHAPTER VII	41
CHAPTER VIII	45
CHAPTER IX	50
CHAPTER X	53
CHAPTER XI	57
CHAPTER XII	60
CHAPTER XIII	64
CHAPTER XIV	68
CHAPTER XV	71
CHAPTER XVI	75

BOOK FOUR : 1806

CHAPTER I

Early in the year 1806 Nicholas Rostóv returned home on leave. Denísov was going home to Vorónezh and Rostóv persuaded him to travel with him as far as Moscow and to stay with him there. Meeting a comrade at the last post station but one before Moscow, Denísov had drunk three bottles of wine with him and, despite the jolting ruts across the snow-covered road, did not once wake up on the way to Moscow, but lay at the bottom of the sleigh beside Rostóv, who grew more and more impatient the nearer they got to Moscow.

"How much longer? How much longer? Oh, these insufferable streets, shops, bakers' signboards, street lamps, and sleighs!" thought Rostóv, when their leave permits had been passed at the town gate and they had entered Moscow.

"Denísov! We're here! He's asleep," he added, leaning forward with his whole body as if in that position he hoped to hasten the speed of the sleigh.

Denísov gave no answer.

"There's the corner at the crossroads, where the cabman, Zakhár, has his stand, and there's Zakhár himself and still the same horse! And here's the little shop where we used to buy gingerbread! Can't you hurry up? Now then!"

"Which house is it?" asked the driver.

"Why, that one, right at the end, the big one. Don't you see? That's our house," said Rostóv. "Of course, it's our house! Denísov, Denísov! We're almost there!"

Denísov raised his head, coughed, and made no answer.

"Dmítri," said Rostóv to his valet on the box, "those lights are in our house, aren't they?"

"Yes, sir, and there's a light in your father's study."

"Then they've not gone to bed yet? What do you think? Mind now, don't forget to put out my new coat," added Rostóv, fingering his new mustache. "Now then, get on," he shouted to the driver. "Do wake up, Váska!" he went on, turning to Denísov, whose head was again nodding. "Come, get on! You shall have three rubles for vodka—get on!" Rostóv shouted, when the sleigh was only three houses from his door. It seemed to him the horses were not moving at all. At last the sleigh bore to the right, drew up at an entrance, and Rostóv saw overhead the old familiar cornice with a bit of plaster broken off, the porch, and the post by the side of the pavement. He sprang out before the sleigh stopped, and ran into the hall. The house stood cold and silent, as if quite regardless of who had come to it. There was no one in the hall. "Oh God! Is everyone all right?" he thought, stopping for a moment with a sinking heart, and then immediately starting to run along the hall and up the warped steps of the familiar staircase. The well-known old door handle, which always angered the countess when it was not properly cleaned, turned as loosely as ever. A solitary tallow candle burned in the anteroom.

Old Michael was asleep on the chest. Prokófy, the footman, who was so strong that he could lift the back of the carriage from behind, sat plaiting slippers out of cloth selvedges. He looked up at the opening door and his expression of sleepy indifference suddenly changed to one of delighted amazement.

"Gracious heavens! The young count!" he cried, recognizing his young master. "Can it be? My treasure!" and Prokófy, trembling with excitement, rushed toward the drawing room door, probably in order to announce him, but, changing his mind, came back and stooped to kiss the young man's shoulder.

"All well?" asked Rostóv, drawing away his arm.

"Yes, God be thanked! Yes! They've just finished supper. Let me have a look at you, your excellency."

"Is everything quite all right?"

"The Lord be thanked, yes!"

Rostóv, who had completely forgotten Denísov, not wishing anyone to forestall him, threw off his fur coat and ran on tiptoe through the large dark ballroom. All was the same: there were the same old card tables and the same chandelier with a cover over it; but someone had already seen the young master, and, before he had reached the drawing room, something flew out from a side door like a tornado and began hugging and kissing him. Another and yet another creature of the same kind sprang from a second door and a third; more hugging, more kissing, more outcries, and tears of joy. He could not distinguish which was Papa, which Natásha, and which Pétya. Everyone shouted, talked, and kissed him at the same time. Only his mother was not there, he noticed that.

"And I did not know... Nicholas... My darling!..."

"Here he is... our own... Kólya, * dear fellow... How he has changed!... Where are the candles?... Tea!..."

* Nicholas.

"And me, kiss me!"

"Dearest... and me!"

Sónya, Natásha, Pétya, Anna Mikháylovna, Véra, and the old count were all hugging him, and the serfs, men and maids, flocked into the room, exclaiming and oh-ing and ah-ing.

Pétya, clinging to his legs, kept shouting, "And me too!"

Natásha, after she had pulled him down toward her and covered his face with kisses, holding him tight by the skirt of his coat, sprang away and pranced up and down in one place like a goat and shrieked piercingly.

All around were loving eyes glistening with tears of joy, and all around were lips seeking a kiss.

Sónya too, all rosy red, clung to his arm and, radiant with bliss, looked eagerly toward his eyes, waiting for the look for which she longed. Sónya now was sixteen and she was very pretty, especially at this moment of happy, rapturous excitement. She gazed at him, not taking her eyes off him, and smiling and holding her breath. He gave her a grateful look, but was still expectant and looking for someone. The old countess had not yet come. But now steps were heard at the door, steps so rapid that they could hardly be his mother's.

Yet it was she, dressed in a new gown which he did not know, made since he had left. All the others let him go, and he ran to her. When they met, she fell on his breast, sobbing. She could not lift her face, but only pressed it to the cold braiding of his hussar's jacket. Denísov, who had come into the room unnoticed by anyone, stood there and wiped his eyes at the sight.

"VasíliDenísov, your son's friend," he said, introducing himself to the count, who was looking inquiringly at him.

"You are most welcome! I know, I know," said the count, kissing and embracing Denísov. "Nicholas wrote us... Natásha, Véra, look! Here is Denísov!"

The same happy, rapturous faces turned to the shaggy figure of Denísov.

"Darling Denísov!" screamed Natásha, beside herself with rapture, springing to him, putting her arms round him, and kissing him. This escapade made everybody feel confused. Denísov blushed too, but smiled and, taking Natásha's hand, kissed it.

Denísov was shown to the room prepared for him, and the Rostóvs all gathered round Nicholas in the sitting room.

The old countess, not letting go of his hand and kissing it every moment, sat beside him: the rest, crowding round him, watched every movement, word, or look of his, never taking their blissfully adoring eyes off him. His brother and sisters struggled for the places nearest to him and disputed with one another who should bring him his tea, handkerchief, and pipe.

Rostóv was very happy in the love they showed him; but the first moment of meeting had been so beatific that his present joy seemed insufficient, and he kept expecting something more, more and yet more.

Next morning, after the fatigues of their journey, the travelers slept till ten o'clock.

In the room next to their bedroom there was a confusion of sabers, satchels, sabretaches, open portmanteaus, and dirty boots. Two freshly cleaned pairs with spurs had just been placed by the wall. The servants were bringing in jugs and basins, hot water for shaving, and their well-brushed clothes. There was a masculine odor and a smell of tobacco.

"Hallo, Gwíska—my pipe!" came VasíliDenísov's husky voice. "Wostóv, get up!"

Rostóv, rubbing his eyes that seemed glued together, raised his disheveled head from the hot pillow.

"Why, is it late?"

"Late! It's nearly ten o'clock," answered Natásha's voice. A rustle of starched petticoats and the whispering and laughter of girls' voices came from the adjoining room. The door was opened a crack and there was a glimpse of something blue, of ribbons, black hair, and merry faces. It was Natásha, Sónya, and Pétya, who had come to see whether they were getting up.

"Nicholas! Get up!" Natásha's voice was again heard at the door.

"Directly!"

Meanwhile, Pétya, having found and seized the sabers in the outer room, with the delight boys feel at the sight of a military elder brother, and forgetting that it was unbecoming for the girls to see men undressed, opened the bedroom door.

"Is this your saber?" he shouted.

The girls sprang aside. Denísov hid his hairy legs under the blanket, looking with a scared face at his comrade for help. The door, having let Pétya in, closed again. A sound of laughter came from behind it.

"Nicholas! Come out in your dressing gown!" said Natásha's voice.

"Is this your saber?" asked Pétya. "Or is it yours?" he said, addressing the black-mustachedDenísov with servile deference.

Rostóv hurriedly put something on his feet, drew on his dressing gown, and went out. Natásha had put on one spurred boot and was just getting her foot into the other. Sónya, when he came in, was twirling round and was about to expand her dresses into a balloon and sit down. They were dressed alike, in new pale-blue frocks, and were both fresh, rosy, and bright. Sónya ran away, but Natásha, taking her brother's arm, led him into the sitting room, where they began talking. They hardly gave one another time to ask questions and give replies concerning a thousand little matters which could not interest anyone but themselves. Natásha laughed at every word he said or that she said herself, not because what they were saying was amusing, but because she felt happy and was unable to control her joy which expressed itself by laughter.

"Oh, how nice, how splendid!" she said to everything.

Rostóv felt that, under the influence of the warm rays of love, that childlike smile which had not once appeared on his face since he left home now for the first time after eighteen months again brightened his soul and his face.

"No, but listen," she said, "now you are quite a man, aren't you? I'm awfully glad you're my brother." She touched his mustache. "I want to know what you men are like. Are you the same as we? No?"

"Why did Sónya run away?" asked Rostóv.

"Ah, yes! That's a whole long story! How are you going to speak to her—*thou* or *you?*"

"As may happen," said Rostóv.

"No, call her *you*, please! I'll tell you all about it some other time. No, I'll tell you now. You know Sónya's my dearest friend. Such a friend that I burned my arm for her sake. Look here!"

She pulled up her muslin sleeve and showed him a red scar on her long, slender, delicate arm, high above the elbow on that part that is covered even by a ball dress.

"I burned this to prove my love for her. I just heated a ruler in the fire and pressed it there!"

Sitting on the sofa with the little cushions on its arms, in what used to be his old schoolroom, and looking into Natásha's wildly bright eyes, Rostóv re-entered that world of home and childhood which had no meaning for anyone else, but gave him some of the best joys of his life; and the burning of an arm with a ruler as a proof of love did not seem to him senseless, he understood and was not surprised at it.

"Well, and is that all?" he asked.

"We are such friends, such friends! All that ruler business was just nonsense, but we are friends forever. She, if she loves anyone, does it for life, but I don't understand that, I forget quickly."

"Well, what then?"

"Well, she loves me and you like that."

Natásha suddenly flushed.

"Why, you remember before you went away?... Well, she says you are to forget all that.... She says: 'I shall love him always, but let him be free.' Isn't that lovely and noble! Yes, very noble? Isn't it?" asked Natásha, so seriously and excitedly that it was evident that what she was now saying she had talked of before, with tears.

Rostóv became thoughtful.

"I never go back on my word," he said. "Besides, Sónya is so charming that only a fool would renounce such happiness."

"No, no!" cried Natásha, "she and I have already talked it over. We knew you'd say so. But it won't do, because you see, if you say that—if you consider yourself bound by your promise—it will seem as if she had not meant it seriously. It makes it as if you were marrying her because you must, and that wouldn't do at all."

Rostóv saw that it had been well considered by them. Sónya had already struck him by her beauty on the preceding day. Today, when he had caught a glimpse of her, she seemed still more lovely. She was a charming girl of sixteen, evidently passionately in love with him (he did not doubt that for an instant). Why should he not love her now, and even marry her, Rostóv thought, but just now there were so many other pleasures and interests before him! "Yes, they have taken a wise decision," he thought, "I must remain free."

"Well then, that's excellent," said he. "We'll talk it over later on. Oh, how glad I am to have you!"

"Well, and are you still true to Borís?" he continued.

"Oh, what nonsense!" cried Natásha, laughing. "I don't think about him or anyone else, and I don't want anything of the kind."

"Dear me! Then what are you up to now?"

"Now?" repeated Natásha, and a happy smile lit up her face. "Have you seen Duport?"

"No."

"Not seen Duport—the famous dancer? Well then, you won't understand. That's what I'm up to."

Curving her arms, Natásha held out her skirts as dancers do, ran back a few steps, turned, cut a caper, brought her little feet sharply together, and made some steps on the very tips of her toes.

"See, I'm standing! See!" she said, but could not maintain herself on her toes any longer. "So that's what I'm up to! I'll never marry anyone, but will be a dancer. Only don't tell anyone."

Rostóv laughed so loud and merrily that Denísov, in his bedroom, felt envious and Natásha could not help joining in.

"No, but don't you think it's nice?" she kept repeating.

"Nice! And so you no longer wish to marry Borís?"

Natásha flared up. "I don't want to marry anyone. And I'll tell him so when I see him!"

"Dear me!" said Rostóv.

"But that's all rubbish," Natásha chattered on. "And is Denísov nice?" she asked.

"Yes, indeed!"

"Oh, well then, good-by: go and dress. Is he very terrible, Denísov?"

"Why terrible?" asked Nicholas. "No, Váska is a splendid fellow."

"You call him Váska? That's funny! And is he very nice?"

"Very."

"Well then, be quick. We'll all have breakfast together."

And Natásha rose and went out of the room on tiptoe, like a ballet dancer, but smiling as only happy girls of fifteen can smile. When Rostóv met Sónya in the drawing room, he reddened. He did not know how to behave with her. The evening before, in the first happy moment of meeting, they had kissed each other, but today they felt it could not be done; he felt that everybody, including his mother and sisters, was looking inquiringly at him and watching to see how he would behave with her. He kissed her hand and addressed her not as *thou* but as *you—Sónya*. But their eyes met and said *thou*, and exchanged tender kisses. Her looks asked him to forgive her for having dared, by Natásha's intermediacy, to remind him of his promise, and then thanked him for his love. His looks thanked her for offering him his freedom and told her that one way or another he would never cease to love her, for that would be impossible.

"How strange it is," said Véra, selecting a moment when all were silent, "that Sónya and Nicholas now say *you* to one another and meet like strangers."

Véra's remark was correct, as her remarks always were, but, like most of her observations, it made everyone feel uncomfortable, not only Sónya, Nicholas, and Natásha, but even the old countess, who—dreading this love affair which might hinder Nicholas from making a brilliant match—blushed like a girl.

Denísov, to Rostóv's surprise, appeared in the drawing room with pomaded hair, perfumed, and in a new uniform, looking just as smart as he made himself when going into battle, and he was more amiable to the ladies and gentlemen than Rostóv had ever expected to see him.

CHAPTER II

On his return to Moscow from the army, Nicholas Rostóv was welcomed by his home circle as the best of sons, a hero, and their darling Nikólenka; by his relations as a charming, attractive, and polite young man; by his acquaintances as a handsome lieutenant of hussars, a good dancer, and one of the best matches in the city.

The Rostóvs knew everybody in Moscow. The old count had money enough that year, as all his estates had been remortgaged, and so Nicholas, acquiring a trotter of his own, very stylish riding breeches of the latest cut, such as no one else yet had in Moscow, and boots of the latest fashion, with extremely pointed toes and small silver spurs, passed his time very gaily. After a short period of adapting himself to the old conditions of life, Nicholas found it very pleasant to be at home again. He felt that he had grown up and matured very much. His despair at failing in a Scripture examination, his borrowing money from Gavríl to pay a sleigh driver, his kissing Sónya on the sly—he now recalled all this as childishness he had left immeasurably behind. Now he was a lieutenant of hussars, in a jacket laced with silver, and wearing the Cross of St. George, awarded to soldiers for bravery in action, and in the company of well-known, elderly, and respected racing men was training a trotter of his own for a race. He knew a lady on one of the boulevards whom he visited of an evening. He led the mazurka at the Arkhárovs' ball, talked about the war with Field Marshal Kámenski, visited the English Club, and was on intimate terms with a colonel of forty to whom Denísov had introduced him.

His passion for the Emperor had cooled somewhat in Moscow. But still, as he did not see him and had no opportunity of seeing him, he often spoke about him and about his love for him, letting it be understood that he had not told all and that there was something in his feelings for the Emperor not everyone could understand, and with his whole soul he shared the adoration then common in Moscow for the Emperor, who was spoken of as the "angel incarnate."

During Rostóv's short stay in Moscow, before rejoining the army, he did not draw closer to Sónya, but rather drifted away from her. She was very pretty and sweet, and evidently deeply in love with him, but he was at the period of youth when there seems so much to do that there is *no time* for that sort of thing and a young man fears to bind himself and prizes his freedom which he needs for so many other things. When he thought of Sónya, during this stay in Moscow, he said to himself, "Ah, there will be, and there are, many more such girls somewhere whom I do not yet know. There will be time enough to think about love when I want to, but now I have no time." Besides, it seemed to him that the society of women was rather derogatory to his manhood. He went to balls and into ladies' society with an affectation of doing so against his will. The races, the English Club, sprees with Denísov, and visits to a certain house—that was another matter and quite the thing for a dashing young hussar!

At the beginning of March, old Count IlyáRostóv was very busy arranging a dinner in honor of Prince Bagratión at the English Club.

The count walked up and down the hall in his dressing gown, giving orders to the club steward and to the famous Feoktíst, the club's head cook, about asparagus, fresh cucumbers, strawberries, veal, and fish for this dinner. The count had been a member and on the committee of the club from the day it was founded. To him the club entrusted the arrangement of the festival in honor of Bagratión, for few men knew so well how to arrange a feast on an open-handed, hospitable scale, and still fewer men would be so well able and willing to make up out of their own resources what might be needed for the success of the fete. The club cook and the steward listened to the count's orders with pleased faces, for they knew that under no other management could they so easily extract a good profit for themselves from a dinner costing several thousand rubles.

"Well then, mind and have cocks' comb in the turtle soup, you know!"

"Shall we have three cold dishes then?" asked the cook.

The count considered.

"We can't have less—yes, three... the mayonnaise, that's one," said he, bending down a finger.

"Then am I to order those large sterlets?" asked the steward.

"Yes, it can't be helped if they won't take less. Ah, dear me! I was forgetting. We must have another entrée. Ah, goodness gracious!" he clutched at his head. "Who is going to get me the flowers? Dmítri! Eh, Dmítri! Gallop off to our Moscow estate," he said to the factotum who appeared at his call. "Hurry off and tell Maksím, the gardener, to set the serfs to work. Say that everything out of the hothouses must be brought here well wrapped up in felt. I must have two hundred pots here on Friday."

Having given several more orders, he was about to go to his "little countess" to have a rest, but remembering something else of importance, he returned again, called back the cook and the club steward, and again began giving orders. A light footstep and the clinking of spurs were heard at the door, and the young count, handsome, rosy, with a dark little mustache, evidently rested and made sleeker by his easy life in Moscow, entered the room.

"Ah, my boy, my head's in a whirl!" said the old man with a smile, as if he felt a little confused before his son. "Now, if you would only help a bit! I must have singers too. I shall have my own orchestra, but shouldn't we get the gypsy singers as well? You military men like that sort of thing."

"Really, Papa, I believe Prince Bagratión worried himself less before the battle of Schön Grabern than you do now," said his son with a smile.

The old count pretended to be angry.

"Yes, you talk, but try it yourself!"

And the count turned to the cook, who, with a shrewd and respectful expression, looked observantly and sympathetically at the father and son.

"What have the young people come to nowadays, eh, Feoktíst?" said he. "Laughing at us old fellows!"

"That's so, your excellency, all they have to do is to eat a good dinner, but providing it and serving it all up, that's not their business!"

"That's it, that's it!" exclaimed the count, and gaily seizing his son by both hands, he cried, "Now I've got you, so take the sleigh and pair at once, and go to Bezúkhov's, and tell him 'Count Ilyá has sent you to ask for strawberries and fresh pineapples.' We can't get them from anyone else. He's not there himself, so you'll have to go in and ask the princesses; and from there go on to the Rasgulyáy—the coachman Ipátka knows—and look up the gypsy Ilyúshka, the one who danced at Count Orlóv's, you remember, in a white Cossack coat, and bring him along to me."

"And am I to bring the gypsy girls along with him?" asked Nicholas, laughing. "Dear, dear!..."

At that moment, with noiseless footsteps and with the businesslike, preoccupied, yet meekly Christian look which never left her face, Anna Mikháylovna entered the hall. Though she came upon the count in his dressing gown every day, he invariably became confused and begged her to excuse his costume.

"No matter at all, my dear count," she said, meekly closing her eyes. "But I'll go to Bezúkhov's myself. Pierre has arrived, and now we shall get anything we want from his hothouses. I have to see him in any case. He has forwarded me a letter from Borís. Thank God, Borís is now on the staff."

The count was delighted at Anna Mikháylovna's taking upon herself one of his commissions and ordered the small closed carriage for her.

"Tell Bezúkhov to come. I'll put his name down. Is his wife with him?" he asked.

Anna Mikháylovna turned up her eyes, and profound sadness was depicted on her face.

"Ah, my dear friend, he is very unfortunate," she said. "If what we hear is true, it is dreadful. How little we dreamed of such a thing when we were rejoicing at his happiness! And such a lofty angelic soul as young Bezúkhov! Yes, I pity him from my heart, and shall try to give him what consolation I can."

"Wh-what is the matter?" asked both the young and old Rostóv.

Anna Mikháylovna sighed deeply.

"Dólokhov, Mary Ivánovna's son," she said in a mysterious whisper, "has compromised her completely, they say. Pierre took him up, invited him to his house in Petersburg, and now... she has come here and that daredevil after her!" said Anna Mikháylovna, wishing to show her sympathy for Pierre, but by involuntary intonations and a half smile betraying her sympathy for the "daredevil," as she called Dólokhov. "They say Pierre is quite broken by his misfortune."

"Dear, dear! But still tell him to come to the club—it will all blow over. It will be a tremendous banquet."

Next day, the third of March, soon after one o'clock, two hundred and fifty members of the English Club and fifty guests were awaiting the guest of honor and hero of the Austrian campaign, Prince Bagratión, to dinner.

On the first arrival of the news of the battle of Austerlitz, Moscow had been bewildered. At that time, the Russians were so used to victories that on receiving news of the defeat some would simply not believe it, while others sought some extraordinary explanation of so strange an event. In the English Club, where all who were distinguished, important, and well informed foregathered when the news began to arrive in December, nothing was said about the war and the last battle, as though all were in a conspiracy of silence. The men who set the tone in conversation—Count Rostopchín, Prince YúriDolgorúkov, Valúev, Count Markóv, and Prince Vyázemski—did not show themselves at the club, but met in private houses in intimate circles, and the Moscovites who took their opinions from others—IlyáRostóv among them—remained for a while without any definite opinion on the subject of the war and without leaders. The Moscovites felt that something was wrong and that to discuss the bad news was difficult, and so it was best to be silent. But after a while, just as a jury comes out of its room, the bigwigs who guided the club's opinion reappeared, and everybody began speaking clearly and definitely. Reasons were found for the incredible, unheard-of, and impossible event of a Russian defeat, everything became clear, and in all corners of Moscow the same things began to be said. These reasons were the treachery of the Austrians, a defective commissariat, the treachery of the Pole Przebyszéwski and of the Frenchman Langeron, Kutúzov's incapacity, and (it was whispered) the youth and inexperience of the sovereign, who had trusted worthless and insignificant people. But the army, the Russian army, everyone declared, was extraordinary and had achieved miracles of valor. The soldiers, officers, and generals were heroes. But the hero of heroes was Prince Bagratión, distinguished by his Schön Grabern affair and by the retreat from Austerlitz, where he alone had withdrawn his column unbroken and had all day beaten back an enemy force twice as numerous as his own. What also conduced to Bagratión's being selected as Moscow's hero was the fact that he had no connections in the city and was a stranger there. In his person, honor was shown to a simple fighting Russian soldier without connections and intrigues, and to one who was associated by memories of the Italian campaign with the name of Suvórov. Moreover, paying such honor to Bagratión was the best way of expressing disapproval and dislike of Kutúzov.

"Had there been no Bagratión, it would have been necessary to invent him," said the wit Shinshín, parodying the words of Voltaire. Kutúzov no one spoke of, except some who abused him in whispers, calling him a court weathercock and an old satyr.

All Moscow repeated Prince Dolgorúkov's saying: "If you go on modeling and modeling you must get smeared with clay," suggesting consolation for our defeat by the memory of former victories; and the words of Rostopchín, that French soldiers have to be incited to battle by highfalutin words, and Germans by logical arguments to show them that it is more dangerous to run away than to advance, but that Russian soldiers only need to be restrained and held back! On all sides, new and fresh anecdotes were heard of individual examples of heroism shown by our officers and men at Austerlitz. One had saved a standard, another had killed five Frenchmen, a third had loaded five cannon singlehanded. Berg was mentioned, by those who did not know him, as having, when wounded in the right hand, taken his sword in the left, and gone forward. Of Bolkónski, nothing was said, and only those who knew him intimately regretted that he had died so young, leaving a pregnant wife with his eccentric father.

CHAPTER III

On that third of March, all the rooms in the English Club were filled with a hum of conversation, like the hum of bees swarming in springtime. The members and guests of the club wandered hither and thither, sat, stood, met, and separated, some in uniform and some in evening dress, and a few here and there with powdered hair and in Russian *kaftáns*. Powdered footmen, in livery with buckled shoes and smart stockings, stood at every door anxiously noting visitors' every movement in order to offer their services. Most of those present were elderly, respected men with broad, self-confident faces, fat fingers, and resolute gestures and voices. This class of guests and members sat in certain habitual places and met in certain habitual groups. A minority of those present were casual guests—chiefly young men, among whom were Denísov, Rostóv, and Dólokhov—who was now again an officer in the Semënov regiment. The faces of these young people, especially those who were military men, bore that expression of condescending respect for their elders which seems to say to the older generation, "We are prepared to respect and honor you, but all the same remember that the future belongs to us."

Nesvítski was there as an old member of the club. Pierre, who at his wife's command had let his hair grow and abandoned his spectacles, went about the rooms fashionably dressed but looking sad and dull. Here, as elsewhere, he was surrounded by an atmosphere of subservience to his wealth, and being in the habit of lording it over these people, he treated them with absent-minded contempt.

By his age he should have belonged to the younger men, but by his wealth and connections he belonged to the groups of old and honored guests, and so he went from one group to another. Some of the most important old men were the center of groups which even strangers approached respectfully to hear the voices of well-known men. The largest circles formed round Count Rostopchín, Valúev, and Narýshkin. Rostopchín was describing how the Russians had been overwhelmed by flying Austrians and had had to force their way through them with bayonets.

Valúev was confidentially telling that Uvárov had been sent from Petersburg to ascertain what Moscow was thinking about Austerlitz.

In the third circle, Narýshkin was speaking of the meeting of the Austrian Council of War at which Suvórov crowed like a cock in reply to the nonsense talked by the Austrian generals. Shinshín, standing close by, tried to make a joke, saying that Kutúzov had evidently failed to learn from Suvórov even so simple a thing as the art of crowing like a cock, but the elder members glanced severely at the wit, making him feel that in that place and on that day, it was improper to speak so of Kutúzov.

Count IlyáRostóv, hurried and preoccupied, went about in his soft boots between the dining and drawing rooms, hastily greeting the important and unimportant, all of whom he knew, as if they were all equals, while his eyes occasionally sought out his fine well-set-up young son, resting on him and winking joyfully at him. Young Rostóv stood at a window with Dólokhov, whose acquaintance he had lately made and highly valued. The old count came up to them and pressed Dólokhov's hand.

"Please come and visit us... you know my brave boy... been together out there... both playing the hero... Ah, VasíliIgnátovich... How d'ye do, old fellow?" he said, turning to an old man who was passing, but before he had finished his greeting there was a general stir, and a footman who had run in announced, with a frightened face: "He's arrived!"

Bells rang, the stewards rushed forward, and—like rye shaken together in a shovel—the guests who had been scattered about in different rooms came together and crowded in the large drawing room by the door of the ballroom.

Bagratión appeared in the doorway of the anteroom without hat or sword, which, in accord with the club custom, he had given up to the hall porter. He had no lambskin cap on his head, nor had he a loaded whip over his shoulder, as when Rostóv had seen him on the eve of the battle of Austerlitz, but wore a tight new uniform with Russian and foreign Orders, and the Star of St. George on his left breast. Evidently just before coming to the dinner he had had his hair and whiskers trimmed, which changed his appearance for the worse. There was something naïvely festive in his air, which, in conjunction with his firm and virile features, gave him a rather comical expression. Beklesheव and Theodore Uvárov, who had arrived with him, paused at the doorway to allow him, as the guest of honor, to enter first. Bagratión was embarrassed, not wishing to avail himself of their courtesy, and this caused some delay at the doors, but after all he did at last enter first. He walked shyly and awkwardly over the parquet floor of the reception room, not knowing what to do with his hands; he was more accustomed to walk over a plowed field under fire, as he had done at the head of the Kursk regiment at Schön Grabern—and he would have found that easier. The committeemen met him at the first door and, expressing their delight at seeing such a highly honored guest, took possession of him as it were, without waiting for his reply, surrounded him, and led him to the drawing room. It was at first impossible to enter the drawing room door for the crowd of members and guests jostling one another and trying to get a good look at Bagratión over each other's shoulders, as if he were some rare animal. Count IlyáRostóv, laughing and repeating the words, "Make way, dear boy! Make way, make way!" pushed through the crowd more energetically than anyone, led the guests into the drawing room, and seated them on the center sofa. The bigwigs, the most respected members of the club, beset the new arrivals. Count Ilyá, again thrusting his way through the crowd, went out of the drawing room and reappeared a minute later with another committeeman, carrying a large silver salver which he presented to Prince Bagratión. On the salver lay some verses composed and printed in the hero's honor. Bagratión, on seeing the salver, glanced around in dismay, as though seeking help. But all eyes demanded that he should submit. Feeling himself in their power, he resolutely took the salver with both hands and looked sternly and reproachfully at the count who had presented it to him. Someone obligingly took the dish from Bagratión (or he would, it seemed, have held it till evening and have gone in to dinner with it) and drew his attention to the verses.

"Well, I will read them, then!" Bagratión seemed to say, and, fixing his weary eyes on the paper, began to read them with a fixed and serious expression. But the author himself took the verses and began reading them aloud. Bagratión bowed his head and listened:

Bring glory then to Alexander's reign And on the throne our Titus shield. A dreaded foe be thou, kindhearted as a man, A Rhipheus at home, a Caesar in the field! E'en fortunate Napoleon Knows by experience, now, Bagratión, And dare not Herculean Russians trouble...

But before he had finished reading, a stentorian major-domo announced that dinner was ready! The door opened, and from the dining room came the resounding strains of the polonaise:

Conquest's joyful thunder waken, Triumph, valiant Russians, now!...

and Count Rostóv, glancing angrily at the author who went on reading his verses, bowed to Bagratión. Everyone rose, feeling that dinner was more important than verses, and Bagratión, again preceding all the rest, went in to dinner. He was seated in the place of honor between two Alexanders—Bekleshëv and Narýshkin—which was a significant allusion to the name of the sovereign. Three hundred persons took their seats in the dining room, according to their rank and importance: the more important nearer to the honored guest, as naturally as water flows deepest where the land lies lowest.

Just before dinner, Count IlyáRostóv presented his son to Bagratión, who recognized him and said a few words to him, disjointed and awkward, as were all the words he spoke that day, and Count Ilyá looked joyfully and proudly around while Bagratión spoke to his son.

Nicholas Rostóv, with Denísov and his new acquaintance, Dólokhov, sat almost at the middle of the table. Facing them sat Pierre, beside Prince Nesvítski. Count IlyáRostóv with the other members of the committee sat facing Bagratión and, as the very personification of Moscow hospitality, did the honors to the prince.

His efforts had not been in vain. The dinner, both the Lenten and the other fare, was splendid, yet he could not feel quite at ease till the end of the meal. He winked at the butler, whispered directions to the footmen, and awaited each expected dish with some anxiety. Everything was excellent. With the second course, a gigantic sterlet (at sight of which IlyáRostóv blushed with self-conscious pleasure), the footmen began popping corks and filling the champagne glasses. After the fish, which made a certain sensation, the count exchanged glances with the other committeemen. "There will be many toasts, it's time to begin," he whispered, and taking up his glass, he rose. All were silent, waiting for what he would say.

"To the health of our Sovereign, the Emperor!" he cried, and at the same moment his kindly eyes grew moist with tears of joy and enthusiasm. The band immediately struck up "Conquest's joyful thunder waken..." All rose and cried "Hurrah!" Bagratión also rose and shouted "Hurrah!" in exactly the same voice in which he had shouted it on the field at Schön Grabern. Young Rostóv's ecstatic voice could be heard above the three hundred others. He nearly wept. "To the health of our Sovereign, the Emperor!" he roared, "Hurrah!" and emptying his glass at one gulp he dashed it to the floor. Many followed his example, and the loud shouting continued for a long time. When the voices subsided, the footmen cleared away the broken glass and everybody sat down again, smiling at the noise they had made and exchanging remarks. The old count rose once more, glanced at a note lying beside his plate, and proposed a toast, "To the health of the hero of our last campaign, Prince Peter IvánovichBagratión!" and again his blue eyes grew moist. "Hurrah!" cried the three hundred voices again, but instead of the band a choir began singing a cantata composed by Paul IvánovichKutúzov:

Russians! O'er all barriers on! Courage conquest guarantees; Have we not Bagratión? He brings foemen to their knees,... etc.

As soon as the singing was over, another and another toast was proposed and Count IlyáRostóv became more and more moved, more glass was smashed, and the shouting grew louder. They drank to Bekleshëv, Narýshkin, Uvárov, Dolgorúkov, Apráksin, Valúev, to the committee, to all the club members and to all the club guests, and finally to Count IlyáRostóv separately, as the organizer of the banquet. At that toast, the count took out his handkerchief and, covering his face, wept outright.

CHAPTER IV

Pierre sat opposite Dólokhov and Nicholas Rostóv. As usual, he ate and drank much, and eagerly. But those who knew him intimately noticed that some great change had come over him that day. He was silent all through dinner and looked about, blinking and scowling, or, with fixed eyes and a look of complete absent-mindedness, kept rubbing the bridge of his nose. His face was depressed and gloomy. He seemed to see and hear nothing of what was going on around him and to be absorbed by some depressing and unsolved problem.

The unsolved problem that tormented him was caused by hints given by the princess, his cousin, at Moscow, concerning Dólokhov's intimacy with his wife, and by an anonymous letter he had received that morning, which in the mean jocular way common to anonymous letters said that he saw badly through his spectacles, but that his wife's connection with Dólokhov was a secret to no one but himself. Pierre absolutely disbelieved both the princess' hints and the letter, but he feared now to look at Dólokhov, who was sitting opposite him. Every time he chanced to meet Dólokhov's handsome insolent eyes, Pierre felt something terrible and monstrous rising in his soul and turned quickly away. Involuntarily recalling his wife's past and her relations with Dólokhov, Pierre saw clearly that what was said in the letter might be true, or might at least seem to be true had it not referred to *his wife*. He involuntarily remembered how Dólokhov, who had fully recovered his former position after the campaign, had returned to Petersburg and come to him. Availing himself of his friendly relations with Pierre as a boon companion, Dólokhov had come straight to his house, and Pierre had put him up and lent him money. Pierre recalled how Hélène had smilingly expressed disapproval of Dólokhov's living at their house, and how cynically Dólokhov had praised his wife's beauty to him and from that time till they came to Moscow had not left them for a day.

"Yes, he is very handsome," thought Pierre, "and I know him. It would be particularly pleasant to him to dishonor my name and ridicule me, just because I have exerted myself on his behalf, befriended him, and helped him. I know and understand what a spice that would add to the pleasure of deceiving me, if it really were true. Yes, if it were true, but I do not believe it. I have no right to, and can't, believe it." He remembered the expression Dólokhov's face assumed in his moments of cruelty, as when tying the policeman to the bear and dropping them into the water, or when he challenged a man to a duel without any reason, or shot a post-boy's horse with a pistol. That expression was often on Dólokhov's face when looking at him. "Yes, he is a bully," thought Pierre, "to kill a man means nothing to him. It must seem to him that everyone is afraid of him, and that must please him. He must think that I, too, am afraid of him—and in fact I am afraid of him," he thought, and again he felt something terrible and monstrous rising in his soul. Dólokhov, Denísov, and Rostóv were now sitting opposite Pierre and seemed very gay. Rostóv was talking merrily to his two friends, one of whom was a dashing hussar and the other a notorious duelist and rake, and every now and then he glanced ironically at Pierre, whose preoccupied, absent-minded, and massive figure was a very noticeable one at the dinner. Rostóv looked inimically at Pierre, first because Pierre appeared to his hussar eyes as a rich civilian, the husband of a beauty, and in a word—an old woman; and secondly because Pierre in his preoccupation and absent-mindedness had not recognized Rostóv and had not responded to his greeting. When the Emperor's health was drunk, Pierre, lost in thought, did not rise or lift his glass.

"What are you about?" shouted Rostóv, looking at him in an ecstasy of exasperation. "Don't you hear it's His Majesty the Emperor's health?"

Pierre sighed, rose submissively, emptied his glass, and, waiting till all were seated again, turned with his kindly smile to Rostóv.

"Why, I didn't recognize you!" he said. But Rostóv was otherwise engaged; he was shouting "Hurrah!"

"Why don't you renew the acquaintance?" said Dólokhov to Rostóv.

"Confound him, he's a fool!" said Rostóv.

"One should make up to the husbands of pretty women," said Denísov.

Pierre did not catch what they were saying, but knew they were talking about him. He reddened and turned away.

"Well, now to the health of handsome women!" said Dólokhov, and with a serious expression, but with a smile lurking at the corners of his mouth, he turned with his glass to Pierre.

"Here's to the health of lovely women, Peterkin—and their lovers!" he added.

Pierre, with downcast eyes, drank out of his glass without looking at Dólokhov or answering him. The footman, who was distributing leaflets with Kutúzov's cantata, laid one before Pierre as one of the principal guests. He was just going to take it when Dólokhov, leaning across, snatched it from his hand and began reading it. Pierre looked at Dólokhov and his eyes dropped, the something terrible and monstrous that had tormented him all dinnertime rose and took possession of him. He leaned his whole massive body across the table.

"How dare you take it?" he shouted.

Hearing that cry and seeing to whom it was addressed, Nesvítski and the neighbor on his right quickly turned in alarm to Bezúkhov.

"Don't! Don't! What are you about?" whispered their frightened voices.

Dólokhov looked at Pierre with clear, mirthful, cruel eyes, and that smile of his which seemed to say, "Ah! This is what I like!"

"You shan't have it!" he said distinctly.

Pale, with quivering lips, Pierre snatched the copy.

"You...! you... scoundrel! I challenge you!" he ejaculated, and, pushing back his chair, he rose from the table.

At the very instant he did this and uttered those words, Pierre felt that the question of his wife's guilt which had been tormenting him the whole day was finally and indubitably answered in the affirmative. He hated her and was forever sundered from her. Despite Denísov's request that he would take no part in the matter, Rostóv agreed to be Dólokhov's second, and after dinner he discussed the arrangements for the duel with Nesvítski, Bezúkhov's second. Pierre went home, but Rostóv with Dólokhov and Denísov stayed on at the club till late, listening to the gypsies and other singers.

"Well then, till tomorrow at Sokólniki," said Dólokhov, as he took leave of Rostóv in the club porch.

"And do you feel quite calm?" Rostóv asked.

Dólokhov paused.

"Well, you see, I'll tell you the whole secret of dueling in two words. If you are going to fight a duel, and you make a will and write affectionate letters to your parents, and if you think you may be killed, you are a fool and are lost for certain. But go with the firm intention of killing your man as quickly and surely as possible, and then all will be right, as our bear huntsman at Kostromá used to tell me. 'Everyone fears a bear,' he says, 'but when you see one your fear's all gone, and your only thought is not to let him get away!' And that's how it is with me. À demain, moncher." *

* Till tomorrow, my dear fellow.

Next day, at eight in the morning, Pierre and Nesvítski drove to the Sokólniki forest and found Dólokhov, Denísov, and Rostóv already there. Pierre had the air of a man preoccupied with considerations which had no connection with the matter in hand. His haggard face was yellow. He had evidently not slept that night. He looked about distractedly and screwed up his eyes as if dazzled by the sun. He was entirely absorbed by two considerations: his wife's guilt, of which after his sleepless night he had not the slightest doubt, and the guiltlessness of Dólokhov, who had no reason to preserve the honor of a man who was nothing to him.... "I should perhaps have done the same thing in his place," thought Pierre. "It's even certain that I should have done the same, then why this duel, this murder? Either I shall kill him, or he will hit me in the head, or elbow, or knee. Can't I go away from here, run away, bury myself somewhere?" passed through his mind. But just at moments when such thoughts occurred to him, he would ask in a particularly calm and absent-minded way, which inspired the respect of the onlookers, "Will it be long? Are things ready?"

When all was ready, the sabers stuck in the snow to mark the barriers, and the pistols loaded, Nesvítski went up to Pierre.

"I should not be doing my duty, Count," he said in timid tones, "and should not justify your confidence and the honor you have done me in choosing me for your second, if at this grave, this very grave, moment I did not tell you the whole truth. I think there is no sufficient ground for this affair, or for blood to be shed over it.... You were not right, not quite in the right, you were impetuous..."

"Oh yes, it is horribly stupid," said Pierre.

"Then allow me to express your regrets, and I am sure your opponent will accept them," said Nesvítski (who like the others concerned in the affair, and like everyone in similar cases, did not yet believe that the affair had come to an actual duel). "You know, Count, it is much more honorable to admit one's mistake than to let matters become irreparable. There was no insult on either side. Allow me to convey...."

"No! What is there to talk about?" said Pierre. "It's all the same.... Is everything ready?" he added. "Only tell me where to go and where to shoot," he said with an unnaturally gentle smile.

He took the pistol in his hand and began asking about the working of the trigger, as he had not before held a pistol in his hand—a fact that he did not wish to confess.

"Oh yes, like that, I know, I only forgot," said he.

"No apologies, none whatever," said Dólokhov to Denísov (who on his side had been attempting a reconciliation), and he also went up to the appointed place.

The spot chosen for the duel was some eighty paces from the road, where the sleighs had been left, in a small clearing in the pine forest covered with melting snow, the frost having begun to break up during the last few days. The antagonists stood forty paces apart at the farther edge of the clearing. The seconds, measuring the paces, left tracks in the deep wet snow between the place where they had been standing and Nesvítski's and Dólokhov'ssabers, which were stuck into the ground ten paces apart to mark the barrier. It was thawing and misty; at forty paces' distance nothing could be seen. For three minutes all had been ready, but they still delayed and all were silent.

CHAPTER V

"Well, begin!" said Dólokhov.

"All right," said Pierre, still smiling in the same way. A feeling of dread was in the air. It was evident that the affair so lightly begun could no longer be averted but was taking its course independently of men's will.

Denísov first went to the barrier and announced: "As the adve'sawies have wefused a weconciliation, please pwoceed. Take your pistols, and at the word *thwee* begin to advance."

"O-ne! T-wo! Thwee!" he shouted angrily and stepped aside.

The combatants advanced along the trodden tracks, nearer and nearer to one another, beginning to see one another through the mist. They had the right to fire when they liked as they approached the barrier. Dólokhov walked slowly without raising his pistol, looking intently with his bright, sparkling blue eyes into his antagonist's face. His mouth wore its usual semblance of a smile.

"So I can fire when I like!" said Pierre, and at the word "three," he went quickly forward, missing the trodden path and stepping into the deep snow. He held the pistol in his right hand at arm's length, apparently afraid of shooting himself with it. His left hand he held carefully back, because he wished to support his right hand with it and knew he must not do so. Having advanced six paces and strayed off the track into the snow, Pierre looked down at his feet, then quickly glanced at Dólokhov and, bending his finger as he had been shown, fired. Not at all expecting so loud a report, Pierre shuddered at the sound and then, smiling at his own sensations, stood still. The smoke, rendered denser by the mist, prevented him from seeing anything for an instant, but there was no second report as he had expected. He only heard Dólokhov's hurried steps, and his figure came in view through the smoke. He was pressing one hand to his left side, while the other clutched his drooping pistol. His face was pale. Rostóv ran toward him and said something.

"No-o-o!" muttered Dólokhov through his teeth, "no, it's not over." And after stumbling a few staggering steps right up to the saber, he sank on the snow beside it. His left hand was bloody; he wiped it on his coat and supported himself with it. His frowning face was pallid and quivered.

"Plea..." began Dólokhov, but could not at first pronounce the word.

"Please," he uttered with an effort.

Pierre, hardly restraining his sobs, began running toward Dólokhov and was about to cross the space between the barriers, when Dólokhov cried:

"To your barrier!" and Pierre, grasping what was meant, stopped by his saber. Only ten paces divided them. Dólokhov lowered his head to the snow, greedily bit at it, again raised his head, adjusted himself, drew in his legs and sat up, seeking a firm center of gravity. He sucked and swallowed the cold snow, his lips quivered but his eyes, still smiling, glittered with effort and exasperation as he mustered his remaining strength. He raised his pistol and aimed.

"Sideways! Cover yourself with your pistol!" ejaculated Nesvítski.

"Cover yourself!" even Denísov cried to his adversary.

Pierre, with a gentle smile of pity and remorse, his arms and legs helplessly spread out, stood with his broad chest directly facing Dólokhov and looked sorrowfully at him. Denísov, Rostóv, and Nesvítski closed their eyes. At the same instant they heard a report and Dólokhov's angry cry.

"Missed!" shouted Dólokhov, and he lay helplessly, face downwards on the snow.

Pierre clutched his temples, and turning round went into the forest, trampling through the deep snow, and muttering incoherent words:

"Folly... folly! Death... lies..." he repeated, puckering his face.

Nesvítski stopped him and took him home.

Rostóv and Denísov drove away with the wounded Dólokhov.

The latter lay silent in the sleigh with closed eyes and did not answer a word to the questions addressed to him. But on entering Moscow he suddenly came to and, lifting his head with an effort, took Rostóv, who was sitting beside him, by the hand. Rostóv was struck by the totally altered and unexpectedly rapturous and tender expression on Dólokhov's face.

"Well? How do you feel?" he asked.

"Bad! But it's not that, my friend—" said Dólokhov with a gasping voice. "Where are we? In Moscow, I know. I don't matter, but I have killed her, killed... She won't get over it! She won't survive...."

"Who?" asked Rostóv.

"My mother! My mother, my angel, my adored angel mother," and Dólokhov pressed Rostóv's hand and burst into tears.

When he had become a little quieter, he explained to Rostóv that he was living with his mother, who, if she saw him dying, would not survive it. He implored Rostóv to go on and prepare her.

Rostóv went on ahead to do what was asked, and to his great surprise learned that Dólokhov the brawler, Dólokhov the bully, lived in Moscow with an old mother and a hunchback sister, and was the most affectionate of sons and brothers.

CHAPTER VI

Pierre had of late rarely seen his wife alone. Both in Petersburg and in Moscow their house was always full of visitors. The night after the duel he did not go to his bedroom but, as he often did, remained in his father's room, that huge room in which Count Bezúkhov had died.

He lay down on the sofa meaning to fall asleep and forget all that had happened to him, but could not do so. Such a storm of feelings, thoughts, and memories suddenly arose within him that he could not fall asleep, nor even remain in one place, but had to jump up and pace the room with rapid steps. Now he seemed to see her in the early days of their marriage, with bare shoulders and a languid, passionate look on her face, and then immediately he saw beside her Dólokhov's handsome, insolent, hard, and mocking face as he had seen it at the banquet, and then that same face pale, quivering, and suffering, as it had been when he reeled and sank on the snow.

"What has happened?" he asked himself. "I have killed her *lover*, yes, killed my wife's lover. Yes, that was it! And why? How did I come to do it?"—"Because you married her," answered an inner voice.

"But in what was I to blame?" he asked. "In marrying her without loving her; in deceiving yourself and her." And he vividly recalled that moment after supper at Prince Vasíli's, when he spoke those words he had found so difficult to utter: "I love you." "It all comes from that! Even then I felt it," he thought. "I felt then that it was not so, that I had no right to do it. And so it turns out."

He remembered his honeymoon and blushed at the recollection. Particularly vivid, humiliating, and shameful was the recollection of how one day soon after his marriage he came out of the bedroom into his study a little before noon in his silk dressing gown and found his head steward there, who, bowing respectfully, looked into his face and at his dressing gown and smiled slightly, as if expressing respectful understanding of his employer's happiness.

"But how often I have felt proud of her, proud of her majestic beauty and social tact," thought he; "been proud of my house, in which she received all Petersburg, proud of her unapproachability and beauty. So this is what I was proud of! I then thought that I did not understand her. How often when considering her character I have told myself that I was to blame for not understanding her, for not understanding that constant composure and complacency and lack of all interests or desires, and the whole secret lies in the terrible truth that she is a depraved woman. Now I have spoken that terrible word to myself all has become clear.

"Anatole used to come to borrow money from her and used to kiss her naked shoulders. She did not give him the money, but let herself be kissed. Her father in jest tried to rouse her jealousy, and she replied with a calm smile that she was not so stupid as to be jealous: 'Let him do what he pleases,' she used to say of me. One day I asked her if she felt any symptoms of pregnancy. She laughed contemptuously and said she was not a fool to want to have children, and that she was not going to have any children by *me*."

Then he recalled the coarseness and bluntness of her thoughts and the vulgarity of the expressions that were natural to her, though she had been brought up in the most aristocratic circles.

"I'm not such a fool.... Just you try it on.... *Allez-vouspromener*," * she used to say. Often seeing the success she had with young and old men and women Pierre could not understand why he did not love her.

* "You clear out of this."

"Yes, I never loved her," said he to himself; "I knew she was a depraved woman," he repeated, "but dared not admit it to myself. And now there's Dólokhov sitting in the snow with a forced smile and perhaps dying, while meeting my remorse with some forced bravado!"

Pierre was one of those people who, in spite of an appearance of what is called weak character, do not seek a confidant in their troubles. He digested his sufferings alone.

"It is all, all her fault," he said to himself; "but what of that? Why did I bind myself to her? Why did I say *'Je vousaime'* * to her, which was a lie, and worse than a lie? I am guilty and must endure... what? A slur on my name? A misfortune for life? Oh, that's nonsense," he thought. "The slur on my name and honor—that's all apart from myself."

* I love you.

"Louis XVI was executed because they said he was dishonorable and a criminal," came into Pierre's head, "and from their point of view they were right, as were those too who canonized him and died a martyr's death for his sake. Then Robespierre was beheaded for being a despot. Who is right and who is wrong? No one! But if you are alive—live: tomorrow you'll die as I might have died an hour ago. And is it worth tormenting oneself, when one has only a moment of life in comparison with eternity?"

But at the moment when he imagined himself calmed by such reflections, *she* suddenly came into his mind as she was at the moments when he had most strongly expressed his insincere love for her, and he felt the blood rush to his heart and had again to get up and move about and break and tear whatever came to his hand. "Why did I tell her that *'Je vousaime'*?" he kept repeating to himself. And when he had said it for the tenth time, Molière's words: *"Mais que diableallait-il faire dans cettegalère?"* * occurred to him, and he began to laugh at himself.

* "But what the devil was he doing in that galley?"

In the night he called his valet and told him to pack up to go to Petersburg. He could not imagine how he could speak to her now. He resolved to go away next day and leave a letter informing her of his intention to part from her forever.

Next morning when the valet came into the room with his coffee, Pierre was lying asleep on the ottoman with an open book in his hand.

He woke up and looked round for a while with a startled expression, unable to realize where he was.

"The countess told me to inquire whether your excellency was at home," said the valet.

But before Pierre could decide what answer he would send, the countess herself in a white satin dressing gown embroidered with silver and with simply dressed hair (two immense plaits twice round her lovely head like a coronet) entered the room, calm and majestic, except that there was a wrathful wrinkle on her rather prominent marble brow. With her imperturbable calm she did not begin to speak in front of the valet. She knew of the duel and had come to speak about it. She waited till the valet had set down the coffee things and left the room. Pierre looked at her timidly over his spectacles, and like a hare surrounded by hounds who lays back her ears and continues to crouch motionless before her enemies, he tried to continue reading. But feeling this to be senseless and impossible, he again glanced timidly at her. She did not sit down but looked at him with a contemptuous smile, waiting for the valet to go.

"Well, what's this now? What have you been up to now, I should like to know?" she asked sternly.

"I? What have I...?" stammered Pierre.

"So it seems you're a hero, eh? Come now, what was this duel about? What is it meant to prove? What? I ask you."

Pierre turned over heavily on the ottoman and opened his mouth, but could not reply.

"If you won't answer, I'll tell you..." Hélène went on. "You believe everything you're told. You were told..." Hélène laughed, "that Dólokhov was my lover," she said in French with her coarse plainness of speech, uttering the word *amant* as casually as any other word, "and you believed it! Well, what have you proved? What does this duel prove? That you're a fool, *que vousêtes un sot*, but everybody knew that. What will be the result? That I shall be the laughingstock of all Moscow, that everyone will say that you, drunk and not knowing what you were about, challenged a man you are jealous of without cause." Hélène raised her voice and became more and more excited, "A man who's a better man than you in every way..."

"Hm... Hm...!" growled Pierre, frowning without looking at her, and not moving a muscle.

"And how could you believe he was my lover? Why? Because I like his company? If you were cleverer and more agreeable, I should prefer yours."

"Don't speak to me... I beg you," muttered Pierre hoarsely.

"Why shouldn't I speak? I can speak as I like, and I tell you plainly that there are not many wives with husbands such as you who would not have taken lovers (*des amants*), but I have not done so," said she.

Pierre wished to say something, looked at her with eyes whose strange expression she did not understand, and lay down again. He was suffering physically at that moment, there was a weight on his chest and he could not breathe. He knew that he must do something to put an end to this suffering, but what he wanted to do was too terrible.

"We had better separate," he muttered in a broken voice.

"Separate? Very well, but only if you give me a fortune," said Hélène. "Separate! That's a thing to frighten me with!"

Pierre leaped up from the sofa and rushed staggering toward her.

"I'll kill you!" he shouted, and seizing the marble top of a table with a strength he had never before felt, he made a step toward her brandishing the slab.

Hélène's face became terrible, she shrieked and sprang aside. His father's nature showed itself in Pierre. He felt the fascination and delight of frenzy. He flung down the slab, broke it, and swooping down on her with outstretched hands shouted, "Get out!" in such a terrible voice that the whole house heard it with horror. God knows what he would have done at that moment had Hélène not fled from the room.

A week later Pierre gave his wife full power to control all his estates in Great Russia, which formed the larger part of his property, and left for Petersburg alone.

CHAPTER VII

Two months had elapsed since the news of the battle of Austerlitz and the loss of Prince Andrew had reached Bald Hills, and in spite of the letters sent through the embassy and all the searches made, his body had not been found nor was he on the list of prisoners. What was worst of all for his relations was the fact that there was still a possibility of his having been picked up on the battlefield by the people of the place and that he might now be lying, recovering or dying, alone among strangers and unable to send news of himself. The gazettes from which the old prince first heard of the defeat at Austerlitz stated, as usual very briefly and vaguely, that after brilliant engagements the Russians had had to retreat and had made their withdrawal in perfect order. The old prince understood from this official report that our army had been defeated. A week after the gazette report of the battle of Austerlitz came a letter from Kutúzov informing the prince of the fate that had befallen his son.

"Your son," wrote Kutúzov, "fell before my eyes, a standard in his hand and at the head of a regiment—he fell as a hero, worthy of his father and his fatherland. To the great regret of myself and of the whole army it is still uncertain whether he is alive or not. I comfort myself and you with the hope that your son is alive, for otherwise he would have been mentioned among the officers found on the field of battle, a list of whom has been sent me under flag of truce."

After receiving this news late in the evening, when he was alone in his study, the old prince went for his walk as usual next morning, but he was silent with his steward, the gardener, and the architect, and though he looked very grim he said nothing to anyone.

When Princess Mary went to him at the usual hour he was working at his lathe and, as usual, did not look round at her.

"Ah, Princess Mary!" he said suddenly in an unnatural voice, throwing down his chisel. (The wheel continued to revolve by its own impetus, and Princess Mary long remembered the dying creak of that wheel, which merged in her memory with what followed.)

She approached him, saw his face, and something gave way within her. Her eyes grew dim. By the expression of her father's face, not sad, not crushed, but angry and working unnaturally, she saw that hanging over her and about to crush her was some terrible misfortune, the worst in life, one she had not yet experienced, irreparable and incomprehensible—the death of one she loved.

"Father! Andrew!"—said the ungraceful, awkward princess with such an indescribable charm of sorrow and self-forgetfulness that her father could not bear her look but turned away with a sob.

"Bad news! He's not among the prisoners nor among the killed! Kutúzov writes..." and he screamed as piercingly as if he wished to drive the princess away by that scream... "Killed!"

The princess did not fall down or faint. She was already pale, but on hearing these words her face changed and something brightened in her beautiful, radiant eyes. It was as if joy—a supreme joy apart from the joys and sorrows of this world—overflowed the great grief within her. She forgot all fear of her father, went up to him, took his hand, and drawing him down put her arm round his thin, scraggy neck.

"Father," she said, "do not turn away from me, let us weep together."

"Scoundrels! Blackguards!" shrieked the old man, turning his face away from her. "Destroying the army, destroying the men! And why? Go, go and tell Lise."

The princess sank helplessly into an armchair beside her father and wept. She saw her brother now as he had been at the moment when he took leave of her and of Lise, his look tender yet proud. She saw him tender and amused as he was when he put on the little icon. "Did he believe? Had he repented of his unbelief? Was he now there? There in the realms of eternal peace and blessedness?" she thought.

"Father, tell me how it happened," she asked through her tears.

"Go! Go! Killed in battle, where the best of Russian men and Russia's glory were led to destruction. Go, Princess Mary. Go and tell Lise. I will follow."

When Princess Mary returned from her father, the little princess sat working and looked up with that curious expression of inner, happy calm peculiar to pregnant women. It was evident that her eyes did not see Princess Mary but were looking within... into herself... at something joyful and mysterious taking place within her.

"Mary," she said, moving away from the embroidery frame and lying back, "give me your hand." She took her sister-in-law's hand and held it below her waist.

Her eyes were smiling expectantly, her downy lip rose and remained lifted in childlike happiness.

Princess Mary knelt down before her and hid her face in the folds of her sister-in-law's dress.

"There, there! Do you feel it? I feel so strange. And do you know, Mary, I am going to love him very much," said Lise, looking with bright and happy eyes at her sister-in-law.

Princess Mary could not lift her head, she was weeping.

"What is the matter, Mary?"

"Nothing... only I feel sad... sad about Andrew," she said, wiping away her tears on her sister-in-law's knee.

Several times in the course of the morning Princess Mary began trying to prepare her sister-in-law, and every time began to cry. Unobservant as was the little princess, these tears, the cause of which she did not understand, agitated her. She said nothing but looked about uneasily as if in search of something. Before dinner the old prince, of whom she was always afraid, came into her room with a peculiarly restless and malign expression and went out again without saying a word. She looked at Princess Mary, then sat thinking for a while with that expression of attention to something within her that is only seen in pregnant women, and suddenly began to cry.

"Has anything come from Andrew?" she asked.

"No, you know it's too soon for news. But my father is anxious and I feel afraid."

"So there's nothing?"

"Nothing," answered Princess Mary, looking firmly with her radiant eyes at her sister-in-law.

She had determined not to tell her and persuaded her father to hide the terrible news from her till after her confinement, which was expected within a few days. Princess Mary and the old prince each bore and hid their grief in their own way. The old prince would not cherish any hope: he made up his mind that Prince Andrew had been killed, and though he sent an official to Austria to seek for traces of his son, he ordered a monument from Moscow which he intended to erect in his own garden to his memory, and he told everybody that his son had been killed. He tried not to change his former way of life, but his strength failed him. He walked less, ate less, slept less, and became weaker every day. Princess Mary hoped. She prayed for her brother as living and was always awaiting news of his return.

CHAPTER VIII

"Dearest," said the little princess after breakfast on the morning of the nineteenth March, and her downy little lip rose from old habit, but as sorrow was manifest in every smile, the sound of every word, and even every footstep in that house since the terrible news had come, so now the smile of the little princess—influenced by the general mood though without knowing its cause—was such as to remind one still more of the general sorrow.

"Dearest, I'm afraid this morning's *fruschtique* *—as Fóka the cook calls it—has disagreed with me."

* Frühstück: breakfast.

"What is the matter with you, my darling? You look pale. Oh, you are very pale!" said Princess Mary in alarm, running with her soft, ponderous steps up to her sister-in-law.

"Your excellency, should not Mary Bogdánovna be sent for?" said one of the maids who was present. (Mary Bogdánovna was a midwife from the neighboring town, who had been at Bald Hills for the last fortnight.)

"Oh yes," assented Princess Mary, "perhaps that's it. I'll go. Courage, my angel." She kissed Lise and was about to leave the room.

"Oh, no, no!" And besides the pallor and the physical suffering on the little princess' face, an expression of childish fear of inevitable pain showed itself.

"No, it's only indigestion?... Say it's only indigestion, say so, Mary! Say..." And the little princess began to cry capriciously like a suffering child and to wring her little hands even with some affection. Princess Mary ran out of the room to fetch Mary Bogdánovna.

"*Mon Dieu! Mon Dieu!* Oh!" she heard as she left the room.

The midwife was already on her way to meet her, rubbing her small, plump white hands with an air of calm importance.

"Mary Bogdánovna, I think it's beginning!" said Princess Mary looking at the midwife with wide-open eyes of alarm.

"Well, the Lord be thanked, Princess," said Mary Bogdánovna, not hastening her steps. "You young ladies should not know anything about it."

"But how is it the doctor from Moscow is not here yet?" said the princess. (In accordance with Lise's and Prince Andrew's wishes they had sent in good time to Moscow for a doctor and were expecting him at any moment.)

"No matter, Princess, don't be alarmed," said Mary Bogdánovna. "We'll manage very well without a doctor."

Five minutes later Princess Mary from her room heard something heavy being carried by. She looked out. The men servants were carrying the large leather sofa from Prince Andrew's study into the bedroom. On their faces was a quiet and solemn look.

Princess Mary sat alone in her room listening to the sounds in the house, now and then opening her door when someone passed and watching what was going on in the passage. Some women passing with quiet steps in and out of the bedroom glanced at the princess and turned away. She did not venture to ask any questions, and shut the door again, now sitting down in her easy chair, now taking her prayer book, now kneeling before the icon stand. To her surprise and distress she found that her prayers did not calm her excitement. Suddenly her door opened softly and her old nurse, PraskóvyaSávishna, who hardly ever came to that room as the old prince had forbidden it, appeared on the threshold with a shawl round her head.

"I've come to sit with you a bit, Másha," said the nurse, "and here I've brought the prince's wedding candles to light before his saint, my angel," she said with a sigh.

"Oh, nurse, I'm so glad!"

"God is merciful, birdie."

The nurse lit the gilt candles before the icons and sat down by the door with her knitting. Princess Mary took a book and began reading. Only when footsteps or voices were heard did they look at one another, the princess anxious and inquiring, the nurse encouraging. Everyone in the house was dominated by the same feeling that Princess Mary experienced as she sat in her room. But owing to the superstition that the fewer the people who know of it the less a woman in travail suffers, everyone tried to pretend not to know; no one spoke of it, but apart from the ordinary staid and respectful good manners habitual in the prince's household, a common anxiety, a softening of the heart, and a consciousness that something great and mysterious was being accomplished at that moment made itself felt.

There was no laughter in the maids' large hall. In the men servants' hall all sat waiting, silently and alert. In the outlying serfs' quarters torches and candles were burning and no one slept. The old prince, stepping on his heels, paced up and down his study and sent Tíkhon to ask Mary Bogdánovna what news.—"Say only that 'the prince told me to ask,' and come and tell me her answer."

"Inform the prince that labor has begun," said Mary Bogdánovna, giving the messenger a significant look.

Tíkhon went and told the prince.

"Very good!" said the prince closing the door behind him, and Tíkhon did not hear the slightest sound from the study after that.

After a while he re-entered it as if to snuff the candles, and, seeing the prince was lying on the sofa, looked at him, noticed his perturbed face, shook his head, and going up to him silently kissed him on the shoulder and left the room without snuffing the candles or saying why he had entered. The most solemn mystery in the world continued its course. Evening passed, night came, and the feeling of suspense and softening of heart in the presence of the unfathomable did not lessen but increased. No one slept.

It was one of those March nights when winter seems to wish to resume its sway and scatters its last snows and storms with desperate fury. A relay of horses had been sent up the highroad to meet the German doctor from Moscow who was expected every moment, and men on horseback with lanterns were sent to the crossroads to guide him over the country road with its hollows and snow-covered pools of water.

Princess Mary had long since put aside her book: she sat silent, her luminous eyes fixed on her nurse's wrinkled face (every line of which she knew so well), on the lock of gray hair that escaped from under the kerchief, and the loose skin that hung under her chin.

Nurse Sávishna, knitting in hand, was telling in low tones, scarcely hearing or understanding her own words, what she had told hundreds of times before: how the late princess had given birth to Princess Mary in Kishenëv with only a Moldavian peasant woman to help instead of a midwife.

"God is merciful, doctors are never needed," she said.

Suddenly a gust of wind beat violently against the casement of the window, from which the double frame had been removed (by order of the prince, one window frame was removed in each room as soon as the larks returned), and, forcing open a loosely closed latch, set the damask curtain flapping and blew out the candle with its chill, snowy draft. Princess Mary shuddered; her nurse, putting down the stocking she was knitting, went to the window and leaning out tried to catch the open casement. The cold wind flapped the ends of her kerchief and her loose locks of gray hair.

"Princess, my dear, there's someone driving up the avenue!" she said, holding the casement and not closing it. "With lanterns. Most likely the doctor."

"Oh, my God! thank God!" said Princess Mary. "I must go and meet him, he does not know Russian."

Princess Mary threw a shawl over her head and ran to meet the newcomer. As she was crossing the anteroom she saw through the window a carriage with lanterns, standing at the entrance. She went out on the stairs. On a banister post stood a tallow candle which guttered in the draft. On the landing below, Philip, the footman, stood looking scared and holding another candle. Still lower, beyond the turn of the staircase, one could hear the footstep of someone in thick felt boots, and a voice that seemed familiar to Princess Mary was saying something.

"Thank God!" said the voice. "And Father?"

"Gone to bed," replied the voice of Demyán the house steward, who was downstairs.

Then the voice said something more, Demyán replied, and the steps in the felt boots approached the unseen bend of the staircase more rapidly.

"It's Andrew!" thought Princess Mary. "No it can't be, that would be too extraordinary," and at the very moment she thought this, the face and figure of Prince Andrew, in a fur cloak the deep collar of which covered with snow, appeared on the landing where the footman stood with the candle. Yes, it was he, pale, thin, with a changed and strangely softened but agitated expression on his face. He came up the stairs and embraced his sister.

"You did not get my letter?" he asked, and not waiting for a reply—which he would not have received, for the princess was unable to speak—he turned back, rapidly mounted the stairs again with the doctor who had entered the hall after him (they had met at the last post station), and again embraced his sister.

"What a strange fate, Másha darling!" And having taken off his cloak and felt boots, he went to the little princess' apartment.

CHAPTER IX

The little princess lay supported by pillows, with a white cap on her head (the pains had just left her). Strands of her black hair lay round her inflamed and perspiring cheeks, her charming rosy mouth with its downy lip was open and she was smiling joyfully. Prince Andrew entered and paused facing her at the foot of the sofa on which she was lying. Her glittering eyes, filled with childlike fear and excitement, rested on him without changing their expression. "I love you all and have done no harm to anyone; why must I suffer so? Help me!" her look seemed to say. She saw her husband, but did not realize the significance of his appearance before her now. Prince Andrew went round the sofa and kissed her forehead.

"My darling!" he said—a word he had never used to her before. "God is merciful...."

She looked at him inquiringly and with childlike reproach.

"I expected help from you and I get none, none from you either!" said her eyes. She was not surprised at his having come; she did not realize that he had come. His coming had nothing to do with her sufferings or with their relief. The pangs began again and Mary Bogdánovna advised Prince Andrew to leave the room.

The doctor entered. Prince Andrew went out and, meeting Princess Mary, again joined her. They began talking in whispers, but their talk broke off at every moment. They waited and listened.

"Go, dear," said Princess Mary.

Prince Andrew went again to his wife and sat waiting in the room next to hers. A woman came from the bedroom with a frightened face and became confused when she saw Prince Andrew. He covered his face with his hands and remained so for some minutes. Piteous, helpless, animal moans came through the door. Prince Andrew got up, went to the door, and tried to open it. Someone was holding it shut.

"You can't come in! You can't!" said a terrified voice from within.

He began pacing the room. The screaming ceased, and a few more seconds went by. Then suddenly a terrible shriek—it could not be hers, she could not scream like that—came from the bedroom. Prince Andrew ran to the door; the scream ceased and he heard the wail of an infant.

"What have they taken a baby in there for?" thought Prince Andrew in the first second. "A baby? What baby...? Why is there a baby there? Or is the baby born?"

Then suddenly he realized the joyful significance of that wail; tears choked him, and leaning his elbows on the window sill he began to cry, sobbing like a child. The door opened. The doctor with his shirt sleeves tucked up, without a coat, pale and with a trembling jaw, came out of the room. Prince Andrew turned to him, but the doctor gave him a bewildered look and passed by without a word. A woman rushed out and seeing Prince Andrew stopped, hesitating on the threshold. He went into his wife's room. She was lying dead, in the same position he had seen her in five minutes before and, despite the fixed eyes and the pallor of the cheeks, the same expression was on her charming childlike face with its upper lip covered with tiny black hair.

"I love you all, and have done no harm to anyone; and what have you done to me?"—said her charming, pathetic, dead face.

In a corner of the room something red and tiny gave a grunt and squealed in Mary Bogdánovna's trembling white hands.

Two hours later Prince Andrew, stepping softly, went into his father's room. The old man already knew everything. He was standing close to the door and as soon as it opened his rough old arms closed like a vise round his son's neck, and without a word he began to sob like a child.

Three days later the little princess was buried, and Prince Andrew went up the steps to where the coffin stood, to give her the farewell kiss. And there in the coffin was the same face, though with closed eyes. "Ah, what have you done to me?" it still seemed to say, and Prince Andrew felt that something gave way in his soul and that he was guilty of a sin he could neither remedy nor forget. He could not weep. The old man too came up and kissed the waxen little hands that lay quietly crossed one on the other on her breast, and to him, too, her face seemed to say: "Ah, what have you done to me, and why?" And at the sight the old man turned angrily away.

Another five days passed, and then the young Prince Nicholas Andréevich was baptized. The wet nurse supported the coverlet with her chin, while the priest with a goose feather anointed the boy's little red and wrinkled soles and palms.

His grandfather, who was his godfather, trembling and afraid of dropping him, carried the infant round the battered tin font and handed him over to the godmother, Princess Mary. Prince Andrew sat in another room, faint with fear lest the baby should be drowned in the font, and awaited the termination of the ceremony. He looked up joyfully at the baby when the nurse brought it to him and nodded approval when she told him that the wax with the baby's hair had not sunk in the font but had floated.

CHAPTER X

Rostóv's share in Dólokhov's duel with Bezúkhov was hushed up by the efforts of the old count, and instead of being degraded to the ranks as he expected he was appointed an adjutant to the governor general of Moscow. As a result he could not go to the country with the rest of the family, but was kept all summer in Moscow by his new duties. Dólokhov recovered, and Rostóv became very friendly with him during his convalescence. Dólokhov lay ill at his mother's who loved him passionately and tenderly, and old Mary Ivánovna, who had grown fond of Rostóv for his friendship to her Fédya, often talked to him about her son.

"Yes, Count," she would say, "he is too noble and pure-souled for our present, depraved world. No one now loves virtue; it seems like a reproach to everyone. Now tell me, Count, was it right, was it honorable, of Bezúkhov? And Fédya, with his noble spirit, loved him and even now never says a word against him. Those pranks in Petersburg when they played some tricks on a policeman, didn't they do it together? And there! Bezúkhov got off scotfree, while Fédya had to bear the whole burden on his shoulders. Fancy what he had to go through! It's true he has been reinstated, but how could they fail to do that? I think there were not many such gallant sons of the fatherland out there as he. And now—this duel! Have these people no feeling, or honor? Knowing him to be an only son, to challenge him and shoot so straight! It's well God had mercy on us. And what was it for? Who doesn't have intrigues nowadays? Why, if he was so jealous, as I see things he should have shown it sooner, but he lets it go on for months. And then to call him out, reckoning on Fédya not fighting because he owed him money! What baseness! What meanness! I know you understand Fédya, my dear count; that, believe me, is why I am so fond of you. Few people do understand him. He is such a lofty, heavenly soul!"

Dólokhov himself during his convalescence spoke to Rostóv in a way no one would have expected of him.

"I know people consider me a bad man!" he said. "Let them! I don't care a straw about anyone but those I love; but those I love, I love so that I would give my life for them, and the others I'd throttle if they stood in my way. I have an adored, a priceless mother, and two or three friends—you among them—and as for the rest I only care about them in so far as they are harmful or useful. And most of them are harmful, especially the women. Yes, dear boy," he continued, "I have met loving, noble, high-minded men, but I have not yet met any women—countesses or cooks—who were not venal. I have not yet met that divine purity and devotion I look for in women. If I found such a one I'd give my life for her! But those!..." and he made a gesture of contempt. "And believe me, if I still value my life it is only because I still hope to meet such a divine creature, who will regenerate, purify, and elevate me. But you don't understand it."

"Oh, yes, I quite understand," answered Rostóv, who was under his new friend's influence.

In the autumn the Rostóvs returned to Moscow. Early in the winter Denísov also came back and stayed with them. The first half of the winter of 1806, which Nicholas Rostóv spent in Moscow, was one of the happiest, merriest times for him and the whole family. Nicholas brought many young men to his parents' house. Véra was a handsome girl of twenty; Sónya a girl of sixteen with all the charm of an opening flower; Natásha, half grown up and half child, was now childishly amusing, now girlishly enchanting.

At that time in the Rostóvs' house there prevailed an amorous atmosphere characteristic of homes where there are very young and very charming girls. Every young man who came to the house—seeing those impressionable, smiling young faces (smiling probably at their own happiness), feeling the eager bustle around him, and hearing the fitful bursts of song and music and the inconsequent but friendly prattle of young girls ready for anything and full of hope—experienced the same feeling; sharing with the young folk of the Rostóvs' household a readiness to fall in love and an expectation of happiness.

Among the young men introduced by Rostóv one of the first was Dólokhov, whom everyone in the house liked except Natásha. She almost quarreled with her brother about him. She insisted that he was a bad man, and that in the duel with Bezúkhov, Pierre was right and Dólokhov wrong, and further that he was disagreeable and unnatural.

"There's nothing for me to understand," she cried out with resolute self-will, "he is wicked and heartless. There now, I like your Denísov though he is a rake and all that, still I like him; so you see I do understand. I don't know how to put it... with this one everything is calculated, and I don't like that. But Denísov..."

"Oh, Denísov is quite different," replied Nicholas, implying that even Denísov was nothing compared to Dólokhov—"you must understand what a soul there is in Dólokhov, you should see him with his mother. What a heart!"

"Well, I don't know about that, but I am uncomfortable with him. And do you know he has fallen in love with Sónya?"

"What nonsense..."

"I'm certain of it; you'll see."

Natásha's prediction proved true. Dólokhov, who did not usually care for the society of ladies, began to come often to the house, and the question for whose sake he came (though no one spoke of it) was soon settled. He came because of Sónya. And Sónya, though she would never have dared to say so, knew it and blushed scarlet every time Dólokhov appeared.

Dólokhov often dined at the Rostóvs', never missed a performance at which they were present, and went to Iogel's balls for young people which the Rostóvs always attended. He was pointedly attentive to Sónya and looked at her in such a way that not only could she not bear his glances without coloring, but even the old countess and Natásha blushed when they saw his looks.

It was evident that this strange, strong man was under the irresistible influence of the dark, graceful girl who loved another.

Rostóv noticed something new in Dólokhov's relations with Sónya, but he did not explain to himself what these new relations were. "They're always in love with someone," he thought of Sónya and Natásha. But he was not as much at ease with Sónya and Dólokhov as before and was less frequently at home.

In the autumn of 1806 everybody had again begun talking of the war with Napoleon with even greater warmth than the year before. Orders were given to raise recruits, ten men in every thousand for the regular army, and besides this, nine men in every thousand for the militia. Everywhere Bonaparte was anathematized and in Moscow nothing but the coming war was talked of. For the Rostóv family the whole interest of these preparations for war lay in the fact that Nicholas would not hear of remaining in Moscow, and only awaited the termination of Denísov's furlough after Christmas to return with him to their regiment. His approaching departure did not prevent his amusing himself, but rather gave zest to his pleasures. He spent the greater part of his time away from home, at dinners, parties, and balls.

CHAPTER XI

On the third day after Christmas Nicholas dined at home, a thing he had rarely done of late. It was a grand farewell dinner, as he and Denísov were leaving to join their regiment after Epiphany. About twenty people were present, including Dólokhov and Denísov.

Never had love been so much in the air, and never had the amorous atmosphere made itself so strongly felt in the Rostóvs' house as at this holiday time. "Seize the moments of happiness, love and be loved! That is the only reality in the world, all else is folly. It is the one thing we are interested in here," said the spirit of the place.

Nicholas, having as usual exhausted two pairs of horses, without visiting all the places he meant to go to and where he had been invited, returned home just before dinner. As soon as he entered he noticed and felt the tension of the amorous air in the house, and also noticed a curious embarrassment among some of those present. Sónya, Dólokhov, and the old countess were especially disturbed, and to a lesser degree Natásha. Nicholas understood that something must have happened between Sónya and Dólokhov before dinner, and with the kindly sensitiveness natural to him was very gentle and wary with them both at dinner. On that same evening there was to be one of the balls that Iogel (the dancing master) gave for his pupils during the holidays.

"Nicholas, will you come to Iogel's? Please do!" said Natásha. "He asked you, and VasíliDmítrich * is also going."

* Denísov.

"Where would I not go at the countess' command!" said Denísov, who at the Rostóvs' had jocularly assumed the role of Natásha's knight. "I'm even weady to dance the *pas de châle*."

"If I have time," answered Nicholas. "But I promised the Arkhárovs; they have a party."

"And you?" he asked Dólokhov, but as soon as he had asked the question he noticed that it should not have been put.

"Perhaps," coldly and angrily replied Dólokhov, glancing at Sónya, and, scowling, he gave Nicholas just such a look as he had given Pierre at the club dinner.

"There is something up," thought Nicholas, and he was further confirmed in this conclusion by the fact that Dólokhov left immediately after dinner. He called Natásha and asked her what was the matter.

"And I was looking for you," said Natásha running out to him. "I told you, but you would not believe it," she said triumphantly. "He has proposed to Sónya!"

Little as Nicholas had occupied himself with Sónya of late, something seemed to give way within him at this news. Dólokhov was a suitable and in some respects a brilliant match for the dowerless, orphan girl. From the point of view of the old countess and of society it was out of the question for her to refuse him. And therefore Nicholas' first feeling on hearing the news was one of anger with Sónya.... He tried to say, "That's capital; of course she'll forget her childish promises and accept the offer," but before he had time to say it Natásha began again.

"And fancy! she refused him quite definitely!" adding, after a pause, "she told him she loved another."

"Yes, my Sónya could not have done otherwise!" thought Nicholas.

"Much as Mamma pressed her, she refused, and I know she won't change once she has said..."

"And Mamma pressed her!" said Nicholas reproachfully.

"Yes," said Natásha. "Do you know, Nicholas—don't be angry—but I know you will not marry her. I know, heaven knows how, but I know for certain that you won't marry her."

"Now you don't know that at all!" said Nicholas. "But I must talk to her. What a darling Sónya is!" he added with a smile.

"Ah, she is indeed a darling! I'll send her to you."

And Natásha kissed her brother and ran away.

A minute later Sónya came in with a frightened, guilty, and scared look. Nicholas went up to her and kissed her hand. This was the first time since his return that they had talked alone and about their love.

"Sophie," he began, timidly at first and then more and more boldly, "if you wish to refuse one who is not only a brilliant and advantageous match but a splendid, noble fellow... he is my friend..."

Sónya interrupted him.

"I have already refused," she said hurriedly.

"If you are refusing for my sake, I am afraid that I..."

Sónya again interrupted. She gave him an imploring, frightened look.

"Nicholas, don't tell me that!" she said.

"No, but I must. It may be arrogant of me, but still it is best to say it. If you refuse him on my account, I must tell you the whole truth. I love you, and I think I love you more than anyone else...."

"That is enough for me," said Sónya, blushing.

"No, but I have been in love a thousand times and shall fall in love again, though for no one have I such a feeling of friendship, confidence, and love as I have for you. Then I am young. Mamma does not wish it. In a word, I make no promise. And I beg you to consider Dólokhov's offer," he said, articulating his friend's name with difficulty.

"Don't say that to me! I want nothing. I love you as a brother and always shall, and I want nothing more."

"You are an angel: I am not worthy of you, but I am afraid of misleading you."

And Nicholas again kissed her hand.

CHAPTER XII

Iogel's were the most enjoyable balls in Moscow. So said the mothers as they watched their young people executing their newly learned steps, and so said the youths and maidens themselves as they danced till they were ready to drop, and so said the grown-up young men and women who came to these balls with an air of condescension and found them most enjoyable. That year two marriages had come of these balls. The two pretty young Princesses Gorchakóv met suitors there and were married and so further increased the fame of these dances. What distinguished them from others was the absence of host or hostess and the presence of the good-natured Iogel, flying about like a feather and bowing according to the rules of his art, as he collected the tickets from all his visitors. There was the fact that only those came who wished to dance and amuse themselves as girls of thirteen and fourteen do who are wearing long dresses for the first time. With scarcely any exceptions they all were, or seemed to be, pretty—so rapturous were their smiles and so sparkling their eyes. Sometimes the best of the pupils, of whom Natásha, who was exceptionally graceful, was first, even danced the *pas de châle*, but at this last ball only the *écossaise*, the *anglaise*, and the mazurka, which was just coming into fashion, were danced. Iogel had taken a ballroom in Bezúkhov's house, and the ball, as everyone said, was a great success. There were many pretty girls and the Rostóv girls were among the prettiest. They were both particularly happy and gay. That evening, proud of Dólokhov's proposal, her refusal, and her explanation with Nicholas, Sónya twirled about before she left home so that the maid could hardly get her hair plaited, and she was transparently radiant with impulsive joy.

Natásha no less proud of her first long dress and of being at a real ball was even happier. They were both dressed in white muslin with pink ribbons.

Natásha fell in love the very moment she entered the ballroom. She was not in love with anyone in particular, but with everyone. Whatever person she happened to look at she was in love with for that moment.

"Oh, how delightful it is!" she kept saying, running up to Sónya.

Nicholas and Denísov were walking up and down, looking with kindly patronage at the dancers.

"How sweet she is—she will be a weal beauty!" said Denísov.

"Who?"

"Countess Natásha," answered Denísov.

"And how she dances! What gwace!" he said again after a pause.

"Who are you talking about?"

"About your sister," ejaculated Denísov testily.

Rostóv smiled.

"My dear count, you were one of my best pupils—you must dance," said little Iogel coming up to Nicholas. "Look how many charming young ladies—" He turned with the same request to Denísov who was also a former pupil of his.

"No, my dear fellow, I'll be a wallflower," said Denísov. "Don't you wecollect what bad use I made of your lessons?"

"Oh no!" said Iogel, hastening to reassure him. "You were only inattentive, but you had talent—oh yes, you had talent!"

The band struck up the newly introduced mazurka. Nicholas could not refuse Iogel and asked Sónya to dance. Denísov sat down by the old ladies and, leaning on his saber and beating time with his foot, told them something funny and kept them amused, while he watched the young people dancing, Iogel with Natásha, his pride and his best pupil, were the first couple. Noiselessly, skillfully stepping with his little feet in low shoes, Iogel flew first across the hall with Natásha, who, though shy, went on carefully executing her steps. Denísov did not take his eyes off her and beat time with his saber in a way that clearly indicated that if he was not dancing it was because he would not and not because he could not. In the middle of a figure he beckoned to Rostóv who was passing:

"This is not at all the thing," he said. "What sort of Polish mazuwka is this? But she does dance splendidly."

Knowing that Denísov had a reputation even in Poland for the masterly way in which he danced the mazurka, Nicholas ran up to Natásha:

"Go and choose Denísov. He is a real dancer, a wonder!" he said.

When it came to Natásha's turn to choose a partner, she rose and, tripping rapidly across in her little shoes trimmed with bows, ran timidly to the corner where Denísov sat. She saw that everybody was looking at her and waiting. Nicholas saw that Denísov was refusing though he smiled delightedly. He ran up to them.

"Please, VasíliDmítrich," Natásha was saying, "do come!"

"Oh no, let me off, Countess," Denísov replied.

"Now then, Váska," said Nicholas.

"They coax me as if I were Váska the cat!" said Denísov jokingly.

"I'll sing for you a whole evening," said Natásha.

"Oh, the faiwy! She can do anything with me!" said Denísov, and he unhooked his saber. He came out from behind the chairs, clasped his partner's hand firmly, threw back his head, and advanced his foot, waiting for the beat. Only on horse back and in the mazurka was Denísov's short stature not noticeable and he looked the fine fellow he felt himself to be. At the right beat of the music he looked sideways at his partner with a merry and triumphant air, suddenly stamped with one foot, bounded from the floor like a ball, and flew round the room taking his partner with him. He glided silently on one foot half across the room, and seeming not to notice the chairs was dashing straight at them, when suddenly, clinking his spurs and spreading out his legs, he stopped short on his heels, stood so a second, stamped on the spot clanking his spurs, whirled rapidly round, and, striking his left heel against his right, flew round again in a circle. Natásha guessed what he meant to do, and abandoning herself to him followed his lead hardly knowing how. First he spun her round, holding her now with his left, now with his right hand, then falling on one knee he twirled her round him, and again jumping up, dashed so impetuously forward that it seemed as if he would rush through the whole suite of rooms without drawing breath, and then he suddenly stopped and performed some new and unexpected steps. When at last, smartly whirling his partner round in front of her chair, he drew up with a click of his spurs and bowed to her, Natásha did not even make him a curtsy. She fixed her eyes on him in amazement, smiling as if she did not recognize him.

"What does this mean?" she brought out.

Although Iogel did not acknowledge this to be the real mazurka, everyone was delighted with Denísov's skill, he was asked again and again as a partner, and the old men began smilingly to talk about Poland and the good old days. Denísov, flushed after the mazurka and mopping himself with his handkerchief, sat down by Natásha and did not leave her for the rest of the evening.

CHAPTER XIII

For two days after that Rostóv did not see Dólokhov at his own or at Dólokhov's home: on the third day he received a note from him:

As I do not intend to be at your house again for reasons you know of, and am going to rejoin my regiment, I am giving a farewell supper tonight to my friends—come to the English Hotel.

About ten o'clock Rostóv went to the English Hotel straight from the theater, where he had been with his family and Denísov. He was at once shown to the best room, which Dólokhov had taken for that evening. Some twenty men were gathered round a table at which Dólokhov sat between two candles. On the table was a pile of gold and paper money, and he was keeping the bank. Rostóv had not seen him since his proposal and Sónya's refusal and felt uncomfortable at the thought of how they would meet.

Dólokhov's clear, cold glance met Rostóv as soon as he entered the door, as though he had long expected him.

"It's a long time since we met," he said. "Thanks for coming. I'll just finish dealing, and then Ilyúshka will come with his chorus."

"I called once or twice at your house," said Rostóv, reddening.

Dólokhov made no reply.

"You may punt," he said.

Rostóv recalled at that moment a strange conversation he had once had with Dólokhov. "None but fools trust to luck in play," Dólokhov had then said.

"Or are you afraid to play with me?" Dólokhov now asked as if guessing Rostóv's thought.

Beneath his smile Rostóv saw in him the mood he had shown at the club dinner and at other times, when as if tired of everyday life he had felt a need to escape from it by some strange, and usually cruel, action.

Rostóv felt ill at ease. He tried, but failed, to find some joke with which to reply to Dólokhov's words. But before he had thought of anything, Dólokhov, looking straight in his face, said slowly and deliberately so that everyone could hear:

"Do you remember we had a talk about cards... 'He's a fool who trusts to luck, one should make certain,' and I want to try."

"To try his luck or the certainty?" Rostóv asked himself.

"Well, you'd better not play," Dólokhov added, and springing a new pack of cards said: "Bank, gentlemen!"

Moving the money forward he prepared to deal. Rostóv sat down by his side and at first did not play. Dólokhov kept glancing at him.

"Why don't you play?" he asked.

And strange to say Nicholas felt that he could not help taking up a card, putting a small stake on it, and beginning to play.

"I have no money with me," he said.

"I'll trust you."

Rostóv staked five rubles on a card and lost, staked again, and again lost. Dólokhov "killed," that is, beat, ten cards of Rostóv's running.

"Gentlemen," said Dólokhov after he had dealt for some time. "Please place your money on the cards or I may get muddled in the reckoning."

One of the players said he hoped he might be trusted.

"Yes, you might, but I am afraid of getting the accounts mixed. So I ask you to put the money on your cards," replied Dólokhov. "Don't stint yourself, we'll settle afterwards," he added, turning to Rostóv.

The game continued; a waiter kept handing round champagne.

All Rostóv's cards were beaten and he had eight hundred rubles scored up against him. He wrote "800 rubles" on a card, but while the waiter filled his glass he changed his mind and altered it to his usual stake of twenty rubles.

"Leave it," said Dólokhov, though he did not seem to be even looking at Rostóv, "you'll win it back all the sooner. I lose to the others but win from you. Or are you afraid of me?" he asked again.

Rostóv submitted. He let the eight hundred remain and laid down a seven of hearts with a torn corner, which he had picked up from the floor. He well remembered that seven afterwards. He laid down the seven of hearts, on which with a broken bit of chalk he had written "800 rubles" in clear upright figures; he emptied the glass of warm champagne that was handed him, smiled at Dólokhov's words, and with a sinking heart, waiting for a seven to turn up, gazed at Dólokhov's hands which held the pack. Much depended on Rostóv's winning or losing on that seven of hearts. On the previous Sunday the old count had given his son two thousand rubles, and though he always disliked speaking of money difficulties had told Nicholas that this was all he could let him have till May, and asked him to be more economical this time. Nicholas had replied that it would be more than enough for him and that he gave his word of honor not to take anything more till the spring. Now only twelve hundred rubles was left of that money, so that this seven of hearts meant for him not only the loss of sixteen hundred rubles, but the necessity of going back on his word. With a sinking heart he watched Dólokhov's hands and thought, "Now then, make haste and let me have this card and I'll take my cap and drive home to supper with Denísov, Natásha, and Sónya, and will certainly never touch a card again." At that moment his home life, jokes with Pétya, talks with Sónya, duets with Natásha, piquet with his father, and even his comfortable bed in the house on the Povarskáya rose before him with such vividness, clearness, and charm that it seemed as if it were all a lost and unappreciated bliss, long past. He could not conceive that a stupid chance, letting the seven be dealt to the right rather than to the left, might deprive him of all this happiness, newly appreciated and newly illumined, and plunge him into the depths of unknown and undefined misery. That could not be, yet he awaited with a sinking heart the movement of Dólokhov's hands. Those broad, reddish hands, with hairy wrists visible from under the shirt cuffs, laid down the pack and took up a glass and a pipe that were handed him.

"So you are not afraid to play with me?" repeated Dólokhov, and as if about to tell a good story he put down the cards, leaned back in his chair, and began deliberately with a smile:

"Yes, gentlemen, I've been told there's a rumor going about Moscow that I'm a sharper, so I advise you to be careful."

"Come now, deal!" exclaimed Rostóv.

"Oh, those Moscow gossips!" said Dólokhov, and he took up the cards with a smile.

"Aah!" Rostóv almost screamed lifting both hands to his head. The seven he needed was lying uppermost, the first card in the pack. He had lost more than he could pay.

"Still, don't ruin yourself!" said Dólokhov with a side glance at Rostóv as he continued to deal.

CHAPTER XIV

An hour and a half later most of the players were but little interested in their own play.

The whole interest was concentrated on Rostóv. Instead of sixteen hundred rubles he had a long column of figures scored against him, which he had reckoned up to ten thousand, but that now, as he vaguely supposed, must have risen to fifteen thousand. In reality it already exceeded twenty thousand rubles. Dólokhov was no longer listening to stories or telling them, but followed every movement of Rostóv's hands and occasionally ran his eyes over the score against him. He had decided to play until that score reached forty-three thousand. He had fixed on that number because forty-three was the sum of his and Sónya's joint ages. Rostóv, leaning his head on both hands, sat at the table which was scrawled over with figures, wet with spilled wine, and littered with cards. One tormenting impression did not leave him: that those broad-boned reddish hands with hairy wrists visible from under the shirt sleeves, those hands which he loved and hated, held him in their power.

"Six hundred rubles, ace, a corner, a nine... winning it back's impossible... Oh, how pleasant it was at home!... The knave, double or quits... it can't be!... And why is he doing this to me?" Rostóv pondered. Sometimes he staked a large sum, but Dólokhov refused to accept it and fixed the stake himself. Nicholas submitted to him, and at one moment prayed to God as he had done on the battlefield at the bridge over the Enns, and then guessed that the card that came first to hand from the crumpled heap under the table would save him, now counted the cords on his coat and took a card with that number and tried staking the total of his losses on it, then he looked round for aid from the other players, or peered at the now cold face of Dólokhov and tried to read what was passing in his mind.

"He knows of course what this loss means to me. He can't want my ruin. Wasn't he my friend? Wasn't I fond of him? But it's not his fault. What's he to do if he has such luck?... And it's not my fault either," he thought to himself, "I have done nothing wrong. Have I killed anyone, or insulted or wished harm to anyone? Why such a terrible misfortune? And when did it begin? Such a little while ago I came to this table with the thought of winning a hundred rubles to buy that casket for Mamma's name day and then going home. I was so happy, so free, so lighthearted! And I did not realize how happy I was! When did that end and when did this new, terrible state of things begin? What marked the change? I sat all the time in this same place at this table, chose and placed cards, and watched those broad-boned agile hands in the same way. When did it happen and what has happened? I am well and strong and still the same and in the same place. No, it can't be! Surely it will all end in nothing!"

He was flushed and bathed in perspiration, though the room was not hot. His face was terrible and piteous to see, especially from its helpless efforts to seem calm.

The score against him reached the fateful sum of forty-three thousand. Rostóv had just prepared a card, by bending the corner of which he meant to double the three thousand just put down to his score, when Dólokhov, slamming down the pack of cards, put it aside and began rapidly adding up the total of Rostóv's debt, breaking the chalk as he marked the figures in his clear, bold hand.

"Supper, it's time for supper! And here are the gypsies!"

Some swarthy men and women were really entering from the cold outside and saying something in their gypsy accents. Nicholas understood that it was all over; but he said in an indifferent tone:

"Well, won't you go on? I had a splendid card all ready," as if it were the fun of the game which interested him most.

"It's all up! I'm lost!" thought he. "Now a bullet through my brain—that's all that's left me!" And at the same time he said in a cheerful voice:

"Come now, just this one more little card!"

"All right!" said Dólokhov, having finished the addition. "All right! Twenty-one rubles," he said, pointing to the figure twenty-one by which the total exceeded the round sum of forty-three thousand; and taking up a pack he prepared to deal. Rostóv submissively unbent the corner of his card and, instead of the six thousand he had intended, carefully wrote twenty-one.

"It's all the same to me," he said. "I only want to see whether you will let me win this ten, or beat it."

Dólokhov began to deal seriously. Oh, how Rostóv detested at that moment those hands with their short reddish fingers and hairy wrists, which held him in their power.... The ten fell to him.

"You owe forty-three thousand, Count," said Dólokhov, and stretching himself he rose from the table. "One does get tired sitting so long," he added.

"Yes, I'm tired too," said Rostóv.

Dólokhov cut him short, as if to remind him that it was not for him to jest.

"When am I to receive the money, Count?"

Rostóv, flushing, drew Dólokhov into the next room.

"I cannot pay it all immediately. Will you take an I.O.U.?" he said.

"I say, Rostóv," said Dólokhov clearly, smiling and looking Nicholas straight in the eyes, "you know the saying, 'Lucky in love, unlucky at cards.' Your cousin is in love with you, I know."

"Oh, it's terrible to feel oneself so in this man's power," thought Rostóv. He knew what a shock he would inflict on his father and mother by the news of this loss, he knew what a relief it would be to escape it all, and felt that Dólokhov knew that he could save him from all this shame and sorrow, but wanted now to play with him as a cat does with a mouse.

"Your cousin..." Dólokhov started to say, but Nicholas interrupted him.

"My cousin has nothing to do with this and it's not necessary to mention her!" he exclaimed fiercely.

"Then when am I to have it?"

"Tomorrow," replied Rostóv and left the room.

CHAPTER XV

To say "tomorrow" and keep up a dignified tone was not difficult, but to go home alone, see his sisters, brother, mother, and father, confess and ask for money he had no right to after giving his word of honor, was terrible.

At home, they had not yet gone to bed. The young people, after returning from the theater, had had supper and were grouped round the clavichord. As soon as Nicholas entered, he was enfolded in that poetic atmosphere of love which pervaded the Rostóv household that winter and, now after Dólokhov's proposal and Iogel's ball, seemed to have grown thicker round Sónya and Natásha as the air does before a thunderstorm. Sónya and Natásha, in the light-blue dresses they had worn at the theater, looking pretty and conscious of it, were standing by the clavichord, happy and smiling. Véra was playing chess with Shinshín in the drawing room. The old countess, waiting for the return of her husband and son, sat playing patience with the old gentlewoman who lived in their house. Denísov, with sparkling eyes and ruffled hair, sat at the clavichord striking chords with his short fingers, his legs thrown back and his eyes rolling as he sang, with his small, husky, but true voice, some verses called "Enchantress," which he had composed, and to which he was trying to fit music:

Enchantress, say, to my forsaken lyre What magic power is this recalls me still? What spark has set my inmost soul on fire, What is this bliss that makes my fingers thrill?

He was singing in passionate tones, gazing with his sparkling black-agate eyes at the frightened and happy Natásha.

"Splendid! Excellent!" exclaimed Natásha. "Another verse," she said, without noticing Nicholas.

"Everything's still the same with them," thought Nicholas, glancing into the drawing room, where he saw Véra and his mother with the old lady.

"Ah, and here's Nicholas!" cried Natásha, running up to him.

"Is Papa at home?" he asked.

"I am so glad you've come!" said Natásha, without answering him. "We are enjoying ourselves! VasíliDmítrich is staying a day longer for my sake! Did you know?"

"No, Papa is not back yet," said Sónya.

"Nicholas, have you come? Come here, dear!" called the old countess from the drawing room.

Nicholas went to her, kissed her hand, and sitting down silently at her table began to watch her hands arranging the cards. From the dancing room, they still heard the laughter and merry voices trying to persuade Natásha to sing.

"All wight! All wight!" shouted Denísov. "It's no good making excuses now! It's your turn to sing the ba'cawolla—I entweat you!"

The countess glanced at her silent son.

"What is the matter?" she asked.

"Oh, nothing," said he, as if weary of being continually asked the same question. "Will Papa be back soon?"

"I expect so."

"Everything's the same with them. They know nothing about it! Where am I to go?" thought Nicholas, and went again into the dancing room where the clavichord stood.

Sónya was sitting at the clavichord, playing the prelude to Denísov'sfavorite barcarolle. Natásha was preparing to sing. Denísov was looking at her with enraptured eyes.

Nicholas began pacing up and down the room.

"Why do they want to make her sing? How can she sing? There's nothing to be happy about!" thought he.

Sónya struck the first chord of the prelude.

"My God, I'm a ruined and dishonored man! A bullet through my brain is the only thing left me—not singing!" his thoughts ran on. "Go away? But where to? It's one—let them sing!"

He continued to pace the room, looking gloomily at Denísov and the girls and avoiding their eyes.

"Nikólenka, what is the matter?" Sónya's eyes fixed on him seemed to ask. She noticed at once that something had happened to him.

Nicholas turned away from her. Natásha too, with her quick instinct, had instantly noticed her brother's condition. But, though she noticed it, she was herself in such high spirits at that moment, so far from sorrow, sadness, or self-reproach, that she purposely deceived herself as young people often do. "No, I am too happy now to spoil my enjoyment by sympathy with anyone's sorrow," she felt, and she said to herself: "No, I must be mistaken, he must be feeling happy, just as I am."

"Now, Sónya!" she said, going to the very middle of the room, where she considered the resonance was best.

Having lifted her head and let her arms droop lifelessly, as ballet dancers do, Natásha, rising energetically from her heels to her toes, stepped to the middle of the room and stood still.

"Yes, that's me!" she seemed to say, answering the rapt gaze with which Denísov followed her.

"And what is she so pleased about?" thought Nicholas, looking at his sister. "Why isn't she dull and ashamed?"

Natásha took the first note, her throat swelled, her chest rose, her eyes became serious. At that moment she was oblivious of her surroundings, and from her smiling lips flowed sounds which anyone may produce at the same intervals and hold for the same time, but which leave you cold a thousand times and the thousand and first time thrill you and make you weep.

Natásha, that winter, had for the first time begun to sing seriously, mainly because Denísov so delighted in her singing. She no longer sang as a child, there was no longer in her singing that comical, childish, painstaking effect that had been in it before; but she did not yet sing well, as all the connoisseurs who heard her said: "It is not trained, but it is a beautiful voice that must be trained." Only they generally said this some time after she had finished singing. While that untrained voice, with its incorrect breathing and laboredtransitions, was sounding, even the connoisseurs said nothing, but only delighted in it and wished to hear it again. In her voice there was a virginal freshness, an unconsciousness of her own powers, and an as yet untrained velvety softness, which so mingled with her lack of art in singing that it seemed as if nothing in that voice could be altered without spoiling it.

"What is this?" thought Nicholas, listening to her with widely opened eyes. "What has happened to her? How she is singing today!" And suddenly the whole world centered for him on anticipation of the next note, the next phrase, and everything in the world was divided into three beats: *"Oh miocrudele affetto."*... One, two, three... one, two, three... One... *"Oh miocrudele affetto."*... One, two, three... One. "Oh, this senseless life of ours!" thought Nicholas. "All this misery, and money, and Dólokhov, and anger, and honor—it's all nonsense... but this is real.... Now then, Natásha, now then, dearest! Now then, darling! How will she take that *si?* She's taken it! Thank God!" And without noticing that he was singing, to strengthen the *si* he sung a second, a third below the high note. "Ah, God! How fine! Did I really take it? How fortunate!" he thought.

Oh, how that chord vibrated, and how moved was something that was finest in Rostóv's soul! And this something was apart from everything else in the world and above everything in the world. "What were losses, and Dólokhov, and words of honor?... All nonsense! One might kill and rob and yet be happy...."

CHAPTER XVI

It was long since Rostóv had felt such enjoyment from music as he did that day. But no sooner had Natásha finished her barcarolle than reality again presented itself. He got up without saying a word and went downstairs to his own room. A quarter of an hour later the old count came in from his club, cheerful and contented. Nicholas, hearing him drive up, went to meet him.

"Well—had a good time?" said the old count, smiling gaily and proudly at his son.

Nicholas tried to say "Yes," but could not: and he nearly burst into sobs. The count was lighting his pipe and did not notice his son's condition.

"Ah, it can't be avoided!" thought Nicholas, for the first and last time. And suddenly, in the most casual tone, which made him feel ashamed of himself, he said, as if merely asking his father to let him have the carriage to drive to town:

"Papa, I have come on a matter of business. I was nearly forgetting. I need some money."

"Dear me!" said his father, who was in a specially good humor. "I told you it would not be enough. How much?"

"Very much," said Nicholas flushing, and with a stupid careless smile, for which he was long unable to forgive himself, "I have lost a little, I mean a good deal, a great deal—forty three thousand."

"What! To whom?... Nonsense!" cried the count, suddenly reddening with an apoplectic flush over neck and nape as old people do.

"I promised to pay tomorrow," said Nicholas.

"Well!..." said the old count, spreading out his arms and sinking helplessly on the sofa.

"It can't be helped! It happens to everyone!" said the son, with a bold, free, and easy tone, while in his soul he regarded himself as a worthless scoundrel whose whole life could not atone for his crime. He longed to kiss his father's hands and kneel to beg his forgiveness, but said, in a careless and even rude voice, that it happens to everyone!

The old count cast down his eyes on hearing his son's words and began bustlingly searching for something.

"Yes, yes," he muttered, "it will be difficult, I fear, difficult to raise... happens to everybody! Yes, who has not done it?"

And with a furtive glance at his son's face, the count went out of the room.... Nicholas had been prepared for resistance, but had not at all expected this.

"Papa! Pa-pa!" he called after him, sobbing, "forgive me!" And seizing his father's hand, he pressed it to his lips and burst into tears.

While father and son were having their explanation, the mother and daughter were having one not less important. Natásha came running to her mother, quite excited.

"Mamma!... Mamma!... He has made me..."

"Made what?"

"Made, made me an offer, Mamma! Mamma!" she exclaimed.

The countess did not believe her ears. Denísov had proposed. To whom? To this chit of a girl, Natásha, who not so long ago was playing with dolls and who was still having lessons.

"Don't, Natásha! What nonsense!" she said, hoping it was a joke.

"Nonsense, indeed! I am telling you the fact," said Natásha indignantly. "I come to ask you what to do, and you call it 'nonsense!'"

The countess shrugged her shoulders.

"If it is true that Monsieur Denísov has made you a proposal, tell him he is a fool, that's all!"

"No, he's not a fool!" replied Natásha indignantly and seriously.

"Well then, what do you want? You're all in love nowadays. Well, if you are in love, marry him!" said the countess, with a laugh of annoyance. "Good luck to you!"

"No, Mamma, I'm not in love with him, I suppose I'm not in love with him."

"Well then, tell him so."

"Mamma, are you cross? Don't be cross, dear! Is it my fault?"

"No, but what is it, my dear? Do you want me to go and tell him?" said the countess smiling.

"No, I will do it myself, only tell me what to say. It's all very well for you," said Natásha, with a responsive smile. "You should have seen how he said it! I know he did not mean to say it, but it came out accidently."

"Well, all the same, you must refuse him."

"No, I mustn't. I am so sorry for him! He's so nice."

"Well then, accept his offer. It's high time for you to be married," answered the countess sharply and sarcastically.

"No, Mamma, but I'm so sorry for him. I don't know how I'm to say it."

"And there's nothing for you to say. I shall speak to him myself," said the countess, indignant that they should have dared to treat this little Natásha as grown up.

"No, not on any account! I will tell him myself, and you'll listen at the door," and Natásha ran across the drawing room to the dancing hall, where Denísov was sitting on the same chair by the clavichord with his face in his hands.

He jumped up at the sound of her light step.

"Nataly," he said, moving with rapid steps toward her, "decide my fate. It is in your hands."

"VasíliDmítrich, I'm so sorry for you!... No, but you are so nice... but it won't do...not that... but as a friend, I shall always love you."

Denísov bent over her hand and she heard strange sounds she did not understand. She kissed his rough curly black head. At this instant, they heard the quick rustle of the countess' dress. She came up to them.

"VasíliDmítrich, I thank you for the honor," she said, with an embarrassed voice, though it sounded severe to Denísov—"but my daughter is so young, and I thought that, as my son's friend, you would have addressed yourself first to me. In that case you would not have obliged me to give this refusal."

"Countess..." said Denísov, with downcast eyes and a guilty face. He tried to say more, but faltered.

Natásha could not remain calm, seeing him in such a plight. She began to sob aloud.

"Countess, I have done w'ong," Denísov went on in an unsteady voice, "but believe me, I so adore your daughter and all your family that I would give my life twice over..." He looked at the countess, and seeing her severe face said: "Well, good-by, Countess," and kissing her hand, he left the room with quick resolute strides, without looking at Natásha.

Next day Rostóv saw Denísov off. He did not wish to stay another day in Moscow. All Denísov's Moscow friends gave him a farewell entertainment at the gypsies', with the result that he had no recollection of how he was put in the sleigh or of the first three stages of his journey.

After Denísov's departure, Rostóv spent another fortnight in Moscow, without going out of the house, waiting for the money his father could not at once raise, and he spent most of his time in the girls' room.

Sónya was more tender and devoted to him than ever. It was as if she wanted to show him that his losses were an achievement that made her love him all the more, but Nicholas now considered himself unworthy of her.

He filled the girls' albums with verses and music, and having at last sent Dólokhov the whole forty-three thousand rubles and received his receipt, he left at the end of November, without taking leave of any of his acquaintances, to overtake his regiment which was already in Poland.